A NAVAJO
LOVE STORY

I0601443

Jon Shirota

TotalRecall Publications, Inc.
1103 Middlecreek
Friendswood, Texas 77546
281-992-3131 281-482-5390 Fax
www.totalrecallpress.com

Printed in the United States of America with simultaneous printing in Australia, Canada, and United Kingdom.

FIRST EDITION
1   2   3   4   5   6   7   8   9   10

In Fond Memories
Of Ramona

Author Bio

Jon Hiroshi Shirota was born on Maui, Hawaii. After serving two years in the U.S. Army, he graduated from Brigham Young University and became an Internal Revenue Agent. He quit his job when he was invited to the Handy Writers Colony in Marshall, Illinois (From Here To Eternity fame) where he finished his first novel Lucky Come Hawaii.

Jon is the recipient of several awards: The John F. Kennedy Center Award; The Rockefeller Center Award; The American College Theater Festival for New Plays; The Best Stage Scenes of 1992 by Smith and Kraus Books; and a grant by the Japan/USA Friendship Commission and the National Endowment for the Arts to spend six months in Okinawa doing research of its immigrants to the United States.

About the Book

Andrea Begayee, an attractive part-Navajo girl, is about to venture out to the world of life. She hasn't decided what college to attend until she meets Mark Kimball, a missionary, who convinces her to attend college with him.

When the young couple met, they had no intention of getting to know each other. Despite their vast differences in race, religion and beliefs they are helplessly pulled together.

Would they have continued their friendly relationship had they known that love does not conquer all, and that the past of one of them will eventually destroy their lives?

Author Note

Reading is learning. Learning is an adventure. An adventure is an invitation that opens up a door to a new horizon. Sometimes, it is a shocking revelation. This, then, is such a story.

Along the southwest and northwest corner of Utah and Arizona is the Navajo reservation. The Navajos are proud independent people. They have become highly educated. And like any other American family who are improving their ways, their lives become complicated.

This is a story of one such modern day family.

Introduction

Andrea... Andrea...

The sun was already beyond the mountains, the long, dark shadows rapidly turning into darkness. The biting, gusty wind was howling through the crevices of the big rocks, the sounds mysterious as ever. It seemed only yesterday when Mark and I were standing here with our backs against the rocks, our hands tight together, our thoughts full of promising tomorrows.

Andrea... Andrea...

The wind continued to blow against our faces, the sound of his voice now near, now far.

Somehow, I knew that my life would never be the same when I met him. It was a weird and strange feeling I had no control over. I tried to understand him, find out why he was so different from other whites. When I finally did, I was already a part of him and he a part of me.

Would it have made any difference had I known from the beginning?

Rejoice, O young man, in thy youth; and let thy heart cheer thee in the days of thy youth, and walk in the ways of thine heart, and in the ways of thine eyes; but know thou, that FOR ALL THESE THINGS God will bring thee into judgement.
--Ecclesiastes, Chapter 11, Verse 9.

CHAPTER 1

The golden sun to my back was sinking beyond the southwestern rim of the Grand Canyon when I braked the brand new '69 Ford pickup beside the two sandy-haired whites walking along the highway. "Want a lift?"

The slender one quickly opened the door and stepped in out of the chilly, early-spring wind. "Thanks a lot," he smiled gratefully.

I waited for his heavy-set companion to get in. "Where are you going?"

"Rainbow City." The slender one slid closer to let his companion shut the door. "Is that where you're going?"

Nodding, I shifted into gear and picked up speed.

"I'm Mark Kimball," said the slender one. "This is Dale Wilkens. We're Mormon missionaries."

I knew who they were when I stopped. Dark-suited Mormon missionaries were always walking along the reservation highways, never thumbing for rides but accepting them when offered.

Mark kept looking at me. "It was getting pretty cold out there," he said, blowing into his hands, rubbing them vigorously. "We're on our way back from Cameron. Is that where you're coming from?"

I shook my head.

"From Flagstaff?" Dale asked.

I shook my head again. I had herded sheep all day with my grandmother in Melon Canyon north of Cameron, and was quite tired. I hoped the missionaries wouldn't attempt a polite conversation.

I kept driving silently through the narrow, winding road towered on both sides by crimson crags and cathedral spires, wondering what Grandma was doing alone in her Hogan. I had wanted to stay with her, but she had insisted that I return home with the fresh pot of lamb stew she had prepared.

"You wouldn't by any chance be a member of our church?" said Mark, hopefully.

"I'm a Presbyterian."

"Oh. A Presbyterian?"

That should stop him. Actually, I did not belong to any church. But a Navajo not belonging to one the churches in the reservation was a potential convert. And jees! There were as many preachers as church goers.

Rainbow City alone had ten different churches. Presbyterian, Methodist, Seventh-Day Adventist, Church of the Brethren, Quaker, Catholic, Christian Reformed Church, Mormon, Massonites and the Plymouth Bretheren Church. Oh, yes, the Navajo Bible Academy.

Eleven!

They were all run by zealous, well-meaning whites, determined to save us pagans from damnation. Some of the God-fearing converts belonged to as many as half-dozen churches.

Although my mother, a half-white, was raised as a Catholic, I grew up with the spiritual beliefs of my paternal grandmother. I learned about the great history of our people from her and about the grim suffering they endured when the Spaniards and later, the Belliganos invaded our land. I also learned about our ceremonial "sing," our chants and our sand painting rituals from her. I was brought up to believe that our people were protected by the four sacred mountains surrounding our land: Big Sheep Peak on the north. Mt. Taylor on the south, San Francisco Peaks on the west and the Pelado Mountains on the east.

"I know who you are!" Dale suddenly snapped his fingers. "You're Andrea Begayee, last year's rodeo queen for the Rainbow City fair. Right?"

I felt myself blushing. I looked everything but a queen at the moment, my face dirty, my long black hair disheveled, my patched jeans and grubby sweater reeking sheep and horse dung.

Mark stared at me, but said nothing.

"I thought you looked familiar," said Dale. "Your picture was in the Navajo Times."

In the white papers, too, I was tempted to tell him.

"You're a bronco rider, right?" said Dale.

The papers had exaggerated it, but I nodded pridefully.

"Ever get hurt riding one of those horses?" Dale asked.

"Naw…" I shrugged. If he did not know that I had given up bronco riding after breaking my arm in the fair rodeo I wasn't about to tell him.

"There must be quite a few Begayees in Rainbow City, too," Mark now said.

I nodded. "Begayees is as common as Smith and Jones."

"Yes, I know," he said.

"Going on to college after high school?" Dale asked.

"NAU," I said. "On a scholarship." He apparently did not know what NAU stood for. "Northern Arizona University," I said.

"Oh, yeah. NAU. Good school. On an academic scholarship?"

I nodded pridefully.

Another round of silence. I thought it was my turn to be polite.

"Where are you from?" I asked.

"Salt Lake City," Mark replied. "Dale's from Las Vegas. We finished a year at the Y before coming on our mission."

"The Y a high school in Utah?" I asked.

"The Y?" Mark laughed. "Brigham Young University. Ever heard of it?"

"Of course," I said. Why didn't he say so in the first place?

"What are you planning on majoring in?" Mark wanted to know.

"Education."

"And teach here in the reservation?"

"In one of the high schools," I said. "It won't be long before all the teachers in the reservation will be Navajos."

"That would be great," he said.

I looked at him. Was he sincere? Or was he like the rest of them who thought Indians were stupid and incapable of learning?

"How long have you been in the reservation?" I asked.

"A year," he said. "We spent most of the time in Holbrook. We'll be in this Area for the rest of our mission."

"How long is that?"

"Another year."

Then go home and tell your people what a great guy you are for spreading the good word among us poor Indians.

At last after driving through miles of barren flatlands with dwarf pines and sage brushes dotting the hillsides, *I* rounded the long bend and came to the Rainbow City intersection where the town's main service station and trading post were. It was windy and the tall trees at the church and school grounds had turned a dull gray from the powdery dusts.

"Are you going back to your church?" I asked.

"It's just down the road," said Mark. "We'll get off at the corner."

"I'm going that way," I said.

Honking my horn, I waved to Johnny at the station and made a sharp right. Johnny looked up from under the hood of a car he was servicing and waved back.

"Your boyfriend?" Mark asked.

"My brother," I said. "He and my father run that station."

"They do any mechanical work?" Dale asked. "Our car's broken down."

"My father is the best mechanic in town," I boasted. I wasn't going to tell him that Dad was the only mechanic in town.

"You don't have to take us all the way down," Mark said.

I had already turned into the dirt road toward the church, a L-shaped white building with a steeple. Their home, a house trailer, was behind the church. Closeby was a fenced-in graveyard.

Dale thanked me when he got off.

Mark slid over to the door and looked at me, his greenish-brown eyes smiling warmly. "Well," he said, "thanks again."

He stepped out and held the door open. "If you're not doing

anything tonight, why don't you drop by? We're having a show, then later dancing."

"I'm going to be busy," I told him. "Thanks anyway."

He shut the door, stood there, and waved.

I swung the pickup around, climbed back up the dirt road and looked into the rearview mirror. He was still standing there. I crossed the highway into the driveway of our home above the church and glanced back. He was rounding the church, looking toward me.

CHAPTER 2

The next time I saw him was two weeks later at our fairground corral.

He had become a hero among the young Mormons in Rainbow City. He had defeated Ray Eagleton, our finalist in the state wrestling championship, and had held my brother, Johnny, to a draw in a boxing match at the gym. Now, he was going to show us what big-time bronco-riding was like.

It was a Saturday afternoon and all of the kids from town were there at the corral on the hillside. I had gone there to tell Johnny that a customer was waiting to have his car serviced. Johnny had gotten out of the Army only three months before and, still restless, spent most of his time at the gym or the corral breaking wild horses. Having been decorated in Vietnam and winning the Division middleweight boxing championship, he thought he should be doing more important things than servicing car.

I joined the others on the fence and waited for Johnny to bring in the horse. It was a big roan. The same one Johnny was having difficulty breaking. Following closeby was Mark. Unlike Johnny who had on riding boots, Levi's and work shirt, he was wearing a pair of loose, light-brown slacks, sneakers and a BYU sweater. As his followers cheered him on, he smiled and waved to them.

I called Johnny. He handed the reins to his friend, Pancho, and came over.

"What?" he said, adjusting the headband that held down his

long, shoulder-length hair.

"Dad wants you to change the oil in Mr. Johnson's car."

"Aw…" he grumbled. "Let him wait."

"Johnny!"

"I'll be over in a few minutes. I wanna see if that white is as good as he thinks he is."

"Dad's waiting."

"Tell him you couldn't find me," he said swaggering off.

I wasn't about to return to the service station without him.

Johnny was still bitter over his experience in Vietnam. As always, the whites had to prove their superiority over the non-whites, he said. They massacred the Vietnamese like they did the Indians.

That, of course, was not the only reason he was bitter against the whites and mistrusted them. A few months after he was drafted, our brother Billy, a year younger than Johnny, had volunteered in the Marines and had gone to Salt Lake City to say goodbye to his girlfriend who had just moved there. The following day, we received a call from the Salt Lake City Police Department. They said that Billy was killed in an accident. We could not believe it! Dad rushed up to Salt Lake City and was told that Billy had been drunk and was crossing against the street light when a car struck him. The police would not give Dad any more information. Not even the driver's name. They said that it was an "open and shut" case. If Dad wanted more information he would have to hire an attorney.

Johnny returned home on an emergency leave to attend Billy's funeral. He was angry with Dad for not finding out what had really happened. He wanted to drive up to Salt Lake City, but was due back in camp.

He still could not believe that Billy was gone. Not even after the funeral. Johnny, who had been very close to Billy, was terribly bitter over the accident. He said that Billy drank a beer or two occasionally, but was not the type to get drunk. What about the driver? he questioned. Did they check to see if he was drunk? Why didn't they at least give his name?

Johnny had vowed that he would get to the bottom of it when returned home from the Army. A few days after his discharge, he drove up to Salt Lake City, determined to know the truth. They not only gave him the same treatment they gave Dad; they said that the accident had happened over two years ago and the records show that Billy was struck by a car while crossing against the street light. They would not give Johnny any more information. When he protested again, they threatened to arrest him for causing a disturbance.

Returning home, Johnny was even more convinced that the driver was someone very influential. He vowed that if it took him the rest of his life, he would find out exactly how Billy was killed and who did it.

The roan was fractious, his dark, fiery eyes darting here and there. Johnny led him to the center and, handing the reins to Mark, held the roan's head and waited for Mark to mount. The roan shied away spiritedly. Johnny held his head tighter and moved along with him until he settled down.

Mark lifted his foot into the stirrup and got up confidently.

"You ready!" Johnny called out.

Mark adjusted the reins and sat firmly in the saddle.

"Ready!"

Johnny let go of the rein's head. The roan squealed and snorted bucking wildly.

Mark went high in the air and was thrown hard on the ground.

The crowd gasped as he lay breathlessly. Then, applauded and cheered when he gathered himself up.

"You can to it, Elder Kimble!" they encouraged. "You can do it!"

Johnny and Pancho chased the roan into a corner.

Catching his breath, Mark wiped the dirt of his slacks and sweater, and staggered toward the fence I was sitting, his eyes glassy.

"You'll right?" I asked, as he leaned against the fence.

"Yeah…" he said, shaking his head, pressing his side. "Yeah, I'm all right…" Then, recognizing me, "Oh, hi…"

"Don't tell me you're going to ride him again."

"Can't do worse than I just did," he said, grinning that boyish grin of his.

"Are you sure you're a bronco rider?"

"I've ridden horses before," he said.

"Wild ones like that roan?"

"Oh," he said, "is that what it is?"

"What did you thinks it was? A jackass?"

"Hey!" Johnny called. "You gonna try again or not?"

I jumped of the fence and stormed over to Johnny. "You trying to get him killed!"

"He's a bronco-riding champion, ain't he?" Johnny grinned.

"He's not more a bronco rider than you're an astronaut," I said. "Can't you see he's doing it just so he wouldn't let the kids down."

Mark came over.

"You're going to ride him!" I said.

"Why not?" He took the reins from Johnny. "It can only kill me."

Johnny shrugged.

"Look," I said. "You want to break your neck it's your business. At least give yourself a chance. Hold the reins tighter and try to ride with the bucking and pitching. Don't fight the rhythm."

He stuck his foot into the stirrup, grasped the saddle and jumped on.

Johnny let go the roan's head and hopped on the fence beside me. "That crazy white," he said, grinning, "he's got more guts than the whole bunch of 'em I knew back in Nam."

That was about the highest compliment I had ever heard Johnny give a white.

Snubbing the reins now, Mark rode the vicious bucking and pitching a second or two longer than before. Just as he was thrown, he kicked the stirrups off and managed to land on his hands and knees.

The roan raced around the corral until Pancho cornered it.

Mark came over unsteadily. "I'm learning to fall better, that's for sure."

Learning to fall better. Jees! Don't missionaries ever swear? If that had been Johnny he'd be cursing all over the place.

"Wanna try again?" Johnny asked.

"I'm willing if that creature is," Mark said, determined.

"Naw," Johnny relented. "You've had enough."

Mark glanced toward his followers. "Well," he said gloomily, "they had a good show anyway."

"Hey," said Johnny, "why'd you tell them you're a bronco rider?"

"Me?" Mark said. "Me a bronco rider?"

"That's what the kids in your church went around saying."

"Oh…" Mark nodded, grinning to himself. "That's what it's all about."

"A big-time bronco rider, that's what you're supposed to be," said Johnny.

Mark laughed. "When one of the kids asked if I could ride a wild horse I told him I used to go to the Nevada deserts and lasso mustangs."

"Lasso mustangs!"

"So help me. That's all I told him." Mark glanced over toward his followers. "I let them down, huh?"

"Aw, hell," said Johnny. "You did okay."

"For a mustang lassoer," I said.

"Hey, Pancho!" Johnny called. "Bring him here."

"You're going to let him ride again!" I protested.

"Naw. Not him," said Johnny. "It's my turn this time."

As Pancho held the roan's neck and Johnny prepared to mount, the crowd broke into a loud applause.

"Atta boy, Johnny! Show him! Ride 'em to a standstill!"

Johnny stuck his feet into the stirrups, kicked them off, something I had never seen him do before.

"Ride 'em, Johnny! Ride 'im!"

The roan lunged, kicked and zigzagged viciously. Another jolting buck and Johnny lost his leverage. He went flying into the air, but managed to land unhurt on the ground.

The crowd was disappointed. The missionary had been on longer.

Getting up, Johnny dusted himself, shaking his head. He gave the crowd a harsh look. "Anyone else wanna try!"

No one volunteered.

"C'mon!" he challenged. "Nothing to it. Just ride it to a standstill."

Everyone remained silent.

"You don't have to try twice like the missionary did. Just once!"

Silence.

"No guts, eh?" He swaggered toward the roan.

CHAPTER 3

Mark came to the service station next day. It was my fathers' day off and I was helping Johnny.

I was still furious at a couple of whites pulling out in a Buick Riviera. They had asked the way to Flagstaff.

"Well," I had said, wiping the windshield, "there are several ways."

"The best way, baby," the driver had said impatiently. "We ain't got all day."

"Oh, the best way," I had said. "That would be that way," pointing eastward.

"Thanks, baby," the driver had winked. "Keep the change."

The tires squealed as the big spender from the East spun the Riviera around.

Mark had come back for the mission car being serviced in the garage by Johnny and had heard me.

"Did I hear you telling him that Flagstaff's that way?" he said.

I avoided his eyes.

"You sent them more than a hundred miles out of their way."

"A hundred miles of beautiful scenery," I said.

I hoped they got lost. They had called me a sexy squaw and had made obscene remarks when I was leaning on the fender and checking the hood.

Stepping into the garage with Mark, I noticed that he was limping. "Your legs still hurt?"

"A little," he said. "You should have told me what it's like to ride one of those horses."

"You didn't ask."

"I asked him," he pointed to Johnny whose head was under the hood of a Toyota. "Nothing to it," he said. "Just get on and hang in there."

Johnny stuck his head out, a screwdriver in his hand.

You know something," he said. "I still don't know why you went through with it."

"Couldn't let my guys down."

"Really thought you could do it, huh?"

"With a little help from the Man above I thought I might just be able to hang in there," said Mark.

"I guess He didn't hear you."

"Sure, He did. He saved me from breaking my neck, didn't He? And He inspired a friend to make me look good before my guys, didn't He?"

"Aw…" Johnny stuck his head back under the hood and worked on the carburetor.

"Your brother always like that?" Mark turned to me.

"The stoic Indian-chief type," I said. "Never says thanks; never accepts thanks."

"Hey," Johnny looked back up from under the hood, "what's this I hear about you getting in a scrap in Flagstaff. I thought you missionaries are supposed to be peaceful, not violent."

"Oh, God…" Mark shook his head. "The next one's going to say that I practically killed the man."

"News travel fast in Navajo land," said Johnny.

"What happened?" I asked Johnny.

"Didn't you hear?" said Johnny. "This peace-loving man of God beat the hell outa couple of guys."

"I was just trying to stop them from beating up someone," said Mark.

"Yeah, sure," Johnny said. "By flattening them."

"They turned on me," said Mark.

"Well, anyway," said Johnny, "you should've let them beat Sam up."

"You know him?" Mark asked.

"Sam?" said Johnny. "He's the lousiest no-good bum in the whole reservation."

"Well, those two whites had no business picking on him," Mark said.

A pickup pulled into the station. I went to fill it up, then returned to the garage.

Johnny had shut the hood and was wiping his hands on a piece of cloth. "Andrea, tell him I don't believe in going to church."

"I don't believe in going to church," I parroted.

"Not you. Me!"

"I thought you're a Presbyterian like Andrea," Mark said to Johnny.

"Like who?"

"—Johnny," I quickly interrupted. "Aren't you taking the car for a test drive?"

"Soon as I get the oil off my hands," he said. "He's trying to get me to come to his church tonight."

"To see a play some of our young members are putting on," said Mark. "You're coming, aren't you?"

"Me?"

"Your brother said you would."

I gave Johnny a murderous look.

"She'll come," he said, stepping into the car.

He backed out before I could say anything.

"We need someone to play the piano," said Mark. "Will you play for us?"

He gave me no choice.

* * * * *

Our red, three-bedroom, studio home near the Mormon church was a great improvement over the tin-roofed shack we used to live in when I was in grade school. We now had running water and indoor bathroom. The only people in our town who lived in stucco homes were the school teachers, government workers and a few businessmen. The others still lived in shacks, mud-thatched Hogans and clapboard homes.

I went home earlier than usual to clean up. After trimming my fingernails and brushing my hair, I changed into a blouse and skirt which drew comments from my mother.

"I was beginning to think I had two sons," she said as I stepped into the living room. "About time you dressed like a girl. Who invited you?

"The Mormons."

"Oh."

It was neither an approval nor a disapproval. At one time, she would have said, "If any of my children is going to church, it'll be the Catholic church."

She must be mellowing in her middle age, I told myself, watching her place her rather squat body on the couch beside my father.

"Johnny worked on the missionary's car?" my father asked.

He was watching the evening news on TV, his bronze complexion seemingly much darker as he sat beside my light-complexioned mother.

"He got through a few minutes ago," I replied.

"If you're in a play, how come you're not inviting your mother and me?" he said.

"Oh, Dad. It's just a kids' play."

"You still could've invited us."

My father was a Marine during World War II. He was one of the code-talkers who distinguished themselves in the Pacific battling the Japanese by speaking Navajo over radios and telephones. After his discharge, Dad went to a trade school in Phoenix on the GI Bill, then worked in a garage before opening his own business in the reservation.

"If we want our children to be educated," he often said to my mother, "we have to take an interest in the system."

The system meant the white man's ways which my mother, a half-white, did not particularly wish upon her children.

"You two want to come," I said, opening the front door, "I'm sure you're welcome."

Mom said nothing.

"We'll be there" said Dad.

✳ ✳ ✳ ✳ ✳

Mark and Dale were already in the recreation room when I arrived. The sliding door adjoining the church in the back was shut and the room was lined up with folding chairs. Up front was a small stage, on one side a piano.

"Glad you could come early," Mark shook my hand, observing my blouse and skirt under my coat. Thought I only wore only jeans, didn't you?

Mark explained what the play was about, then helped me go through my part. About an hour later, the six kids in the play arrived and went to the back to put on make-ups and costumes. Shortly, the room was filled with their friends and families. In the last row were my father and mother eagerly awaiting their daughter's grand debut.

The play was short. It was a reverse stereotype of the wild west. The President of the United States is an Indian. He is confronted with problems of whites attacking Army forts guarded by Indian troops. He sends his emissary to sign a treaty with the whites. No sooner is the treaty signed then the whites raid the forts again. They are desperate. The reservations where they were confined grew nothing and there is no wild games.

I accompanied the kids whenever they sang Western ballads of Indian troops capturing white savages and bringing them to justice. Everyone burst out laughing when the kids referred to the President as the Great Red Father who treated the whites as equals and offered them lots of land with deep blue skies and wide-open spaces.

✳ ✳ ✳ ✳ ✳

"That was the best turn-out we ever had," Mark said, walking me home. "They must have heard you were going to play for us."

Our hands were deep in our pockets, fighting off the freezing night air.

We crossed the highway to our driveway, and stood there looking down at the church it's steeple gleaming under the half-moon. Beyond were the canyons and mesas, faint home lights breaking the silent darkness, scattered car lights creeping up the distant highway. Still beyond were the snow-capped San

Francisco peaks one of our sacred mountains, and directly westward the rim of the Grand Canyon.

"I still can't get over how quiet and peaceful the nights are here," Mark now said. "It's like being in another world.

"It was so quiet the other night I could almost hear the people whispering in their homes down the canyons," he went on.

I remained silent. Was life so different elsewhere?

"I sometimes wonder if we're doing the right thing bringing our ways here," he said.

"May I ask you something?" I now said.

"Sure. Anything."

"Something personal?"

"Sure. Go ahead."

"What made you come here as a missionary?"

He looked at me, his eyes gradually focusing toward the dark meadows.

"I thought this is where I could do the most good," he finally said, his tone mournful and sad.

He kept looking away. He was no longer the zealous missionary with a boyish grin, but a brooding figure suddenly aged.

"You could have gone someplace else?"

"There are thousands of Mormon missionaries all over the world," he said. "We go wherever we're sent."

"You wanted to come here?"

He nodded, his hands still deep in his pockets, his eyes focused distantly. The half-moon disappeared behind gray clouds, then reappeared. A slight breeze came our way, filling the invigorating night air with the pungent fragrance of sages and desert plants.

"Did you come here to tell us your church is better than the others?" I asked, trying not to sound sarcastic.

"I'm here because I believe I have something to offer the people," he finally said.

"Like what?"

"A wonderful way of life."

"Which you think is better than ours?"

"Which I believe The People would enjoy."

"You don't believe we enjoy our ways?" That stumped him.

"We're not trying to replace your ways," he evaded. "We're trying to take the best of your ways and blend them with the best of our ways."

That sounded familiar.

"The Mormons tried to help The People even before the days of the Long Walk," he said.

So, he knows about the long walk.

"Was Kit Carson a Mormon?" I asked.

"Not that I know of."

"Is he a hero of yours?"

"When I was a kid, yes."

"Now?"

"He was no better than the others."

No better than the others! It was Kit Carson and his troops who invaded our nation in the spring of 1863 and virtually starved The People by devastating their corn fields and orchards and burning their homes. Those who managed to escape went to the high mountains and deep canyons where life was unbearable. Others too weak to escape were captured and forced to make the long walk three-hundred and fifty miles to New Mexico where they were held captives for years.

Hundreds perished along the way. Most of them were women and children who were shot by the soldiers because they were too ill and could not keep up with the others.

"Things have changed since those days," said Mark. "And it'll get better."

"For the churches?"

"For the People," he ignored my sarcasm.

And all the credit should go to the churches?

"If you feel so strongly against churches," he said, "why did you claim to be a Presbyterian?"

So, he knew. I wasn't going to apologize.

"I have nothing against churches."

"You do against whites?"

The nerve of him!

"The tourists you meet at the station and the trading posts don't represent most of us, you know."

Did I say that?

"Actually, the tourists that come through here aren't that way when they're back home," he justified. "They're usually tired and irritable by the time they get here."

So, they take it out on us by acting superior, condescending and demanding?

"Ever thought of going to school other than NAU?" he asked, after a passing silence.

"No."

"Don't want to live too far away from home, huh?"

"Why should I?" I said. "I plan to teach right here in the reservation."

"Teach what?" he said. "Things you learn from books?"

Another remark like that and he was going to be standing

there talking to himself.

"Andrea," he was about the place his hand on my shoulder, then dropped it. "The world out there isn't all that bad. I had more reason to be worried coming here than you have going out there. How can you be a good teacher if you're not willing to venture out?"

"I plan to travel one of these days."

"Why not while going to college?"

He's sounding more and more like the rest of them, I thought. A persistent, know-it-all white.

"Ever thought of going to a school like the Y?"

So, that's what he's been leading to. "I'm not a Mormon," I reminded him.

"You don't have to be," he said. "With your scholastic record and recommendation from the President of the mission you won't have trouble getting in."

How long has he been thinking about it?

"There are quite a few Navajos at the Y."

"Aren't they all Mormons?"

"No," he replied. "Not all."

"But they're obligated to join the church."

"No one is obligated to join the church," he said. "The only requirement is that you maintain the standards of the church."

He's got it all figured out, hasn't he?

Since my scholarship from the Tribal Council did not specify what college to attend, I wrote to several colleges. BYU was not one of them. The thought sort of intrigued me now, but I still wasn't going to be talked into it by the know-it-all missionary.

"Think about it," he said. "If you want me to, I'll talk to your father and mother."

"I'll go to whatever school I please," I told him.

A gust of wind suddenly swept up from the canyons and whined through the brushes and rocks above our home.

Mark turned his coat collar up.

I was about to walk off when he extended his hand. "Good night."

Mormons are the most hand-shaking people I ever met, I thought, feeling his hand warm and gentle in mine.

CHAPTER 4

Several days later, I was in the service station office listening to the music on the radio when Dad looked over the newspaper, and said, "That scholarship you got from the tribal council, it says you have to go to NAU?"

"I can go to any school I want," I said.

"Ever thought of going to a school other than NAU?"

"Like where?" I asked, eyeing him."

"Oh, I don't know..." said Dad. "University of Colorado, University of Utah..."

"Or BYU?" I said.

"BYU?" Dad said innocently.

"That Mormon school the missionaries told you about?" I said.

Discovered, Dad looked at me a moment.

"He's right, you know," he now said. "You wanna be a good school teacher you gotta..."

"--Venture out," I said. Damned that missionary.

"Joining the Marines and getting out of the reservation was the best thing happened to me," Dad went on. "No book could've taught me what I learned out there."

"Look what it's done to Johnny," I said.

"He's bitter because of what happened to Billy," he said.

"Aren't you?"

"No matter how you look at it, it still was an accident," he said.

I had always been close to my father. I never thought he

would ever encourage me to leave home. It hurt. Even though I had already written to BYU.

A few days after the long-winded missionary and I had the talk, I went over to our town library and read everything there was on Mormonism and BYU. Surprisingly enough, the librarian was a Mormon and a graduate of the Y. She loaned me some of her own books.

I learned that the Mormons belonged to the Church of Jesus Christ of Latter-Day Saints and that they called themselves LDS. Mormon was derived from the Book of Mormon, the basis for their religion. The missionaries, I read, were mostly young men who volunteered to serve their mission for two years when they became nineteen. They either supported themselves or were supported by their parents while on the mission. Other than special cases, they had no choice where they would be sent.

I wondered why Mark had wanted to come to the Navajo reservation only a few hundred miles away from his home when he could have gone to much more glamorous and exciting places in Europe, South America or Asia.

I was surprised to learn that there was a big Indian Club called the Tribe of Many Feathers at BYU and that the current Miss Indian America was a student there. It intrigued me that the Mormons considered the American Indians as descendants of Laman, a prominent leader in the Book of Mormon. What persuaded me more than anything else to write to the school-- even though I still wasn't sure I wanted to go there--was the discovery that thousands of young Indian kids, mostly Navajos, were living with Mormon families in Utah.

"When I think of it," my father continued, "the people I met out there wasn't too bad."

"For whites," I said.

A car pulled into the garage. It was the Toyota from the Mormon Church. Mark was driving and Dale was beside him.

Mark came running into the office.

"Mr. Begayee," he said, "can we borrow Andrea for a while?"

Dad looked over at me, at Mark.

"We need her for an interpreter."

"Sure," Dad said. "—If it's okay with her."

I gave Mark a cold look. He's asking for it. Oh, is he!

"We're going over to Melon Canyon," he said to me. "To deliver a letter to an elderly couple who can't read."

"Why don't you take one of your church members?" I said. "It would do them good to venture out."

"Andrea!" Dad said sternly. "As long as you're going you can drop this off at your grandmother's," he pushed the package into my arms. "—You don't mind, do you, Mark?"

"Oh, no. Be glad to."

I walked out, said "Hi" to Dale, and got into the back of the Toyota.

Mark exchanged a few words with Johnny in the garage, then joined us.

"Are we all here?" Mark said, expansively, glancing at me, starting the car.

I continued to sit in the back corner, tight-lipped.

"Yep," Mark said, pulling out of the service station, "I guess we're all here."

It was a crisp, early-morning day, the wind hardly blowing, the skies a deep blue and the far-away mountains magnified under the glaring, bright sun.

"Are the passengers in the back comfortable?" Mark said, flippantly.

I remained silent.

"Yep" he said, "I guess they are all very comfortable."

Turning to Dale, he said, "It sure is a nice day, huh, Captain?"

"It sure is, sir," Dale played along. "Extremely nice." Turning around toward me, he said, "Do you know the Williams?"

"Yes," I replied.

"Do you know their son, David?

"No."

"Oh," said Dale, and faced up front again.

After driving silently for about ten minutes, Mark said to Dale, "Do you know how big the reservation is?

"Very big," said Dale.

"How many square miles?"

"Lots," said Dale.

Glancing back over his should, Mark said to me, "Do you know, Andrea?"

I refused to speak to him.

"It's over 25,000 square miles, the size of Vermont, New Hampshire and Massachusetts combined," Mark said. "And there are over 140,000 Navajos living here."

"And we all look alike," I said.

Mark ignored my sarcasm. "Do you know how many miles of paved road we here, Andrea?"

"I haven't bothered to measure them," I said.

"There are over 1,000 miles of paved road," Mark said.

"That's good to know," I said.

"And there are 46 elementary schools, 2 boarding schools,

10-day schools and 8 dormitories on or near the reservation. There are also 6 hospitals, 5 health centers and more than 100 health centers," Mark went on.

"Wow!" Dale went along.

It was my turn. "How many people are there in the state of Utah?" I asked.

"Three-quarters of a million," Mark replied.

"Wrong," I said. "A little over a million. What is the official state flower of Utah?"

Mark looked over at Dale, and they both shrugged.

"It's the sego lily," I informed.

"Is that so?" Mark said.

Dale burst out laughing.

I wasn't about to tell them that I had gotten the information from a tourist guide map.

After driving on for a few more miles, we turned into a powdery dirt road then stopped to let a flock of sheep cross the road. A couple of shaggy dogs were guiding them and a heavily clothed woman on a shaggy horse was bringing up the rear. Mark and Dale waved to the woman. The woman smiled shyly.

We continued on for another five miles, then finally came to Melon Canyon, a scattered settlement along a dry riverbed that stretched for miles between distant cliff walls. Having been there before, Mark went directly to the Williams' home at the foot of a high knoll. Like my grandmother, the Williams lived in a one-room, mud-thatched Hogan. Near the Hogan was a growth of dwarfed cedar tree which seemed to have endured a hard-struggling existence. It reflected the life of Mr. and Mrs. Williams, I thought.

Mr. William was herding sheep into the corral and Mrs.

Williams was outside the Hogan waiting to see who was coming up their road.

"Oh, it is you, Andrea," Mrs. Williams greeted in Navajo as I stepped out. She recognized the missionaries.

"They have a letter for you, Mrs. William," I returned in Navajo.

"From David?" She was excited as Mark handed her the envelope. She called her husband.

Mr. Williams came over, opened the envelope with soiled fingers, and unfolded the letter. His eyes brightened.

"Look," he said to his wife. "Pictures of David."

The missionaries and I stood there, moved by the joy the elderly couple got from the pictures.

"Andrea..." Mr. Williams handed me the letter. "Tell us what David said.

I remembered David Williams. He was about four years older than I and had graduated with honor from our high school. I knew he had gone on to college, but had no idea what school he had chosen.

The letter informed that David would be graduating in May and he would like to have his father and mother there at the commencement.

The elder couple's eyes welled with tears.

"A school teacher..." Mrs. Williams marveled. "Our son a school teacher."

"Andrea," Mark said, "ask them if they can make it for the graduation."

Mr. and Mrs. Williams looked at each other, bewildered.

"What does one wear to those things?" Mrs. Williams asked.

"Wear your traditional blouse and skirt," I suggested. "You

will look very nice them."

"And him? He has no suit."

"He can wear whatever is comfortable."

"We do not want to shame David in front of his university friends," she said.

"Tell her that David will be greatly honored to have his father mother there," said Mark.

I looked at him, surprised.

"I understand a little Navajo," he smiled.

Mr. and Mrs. Williams thought it over.

"If David wants us to be there we will have to go," Mrs. Williams finally decided.

"Good," said Mark. "Tell them we'll write David and let him know exactly when they'll be there. The Indian club will make the necessary arrangements.

Mr. and Mrs. Williams smiled warmly.

✶ ✶ ✶ ✶ ✶

I was no longer angry with Mark as we went back to the car. He was so happy bringing the good news to the elderly couple I couldn't help sharing his happiness.

We drove another mile up the road, then came to Grandma's Hogan at the base of the low mesa. I wondered what Grandma would say, my bringing the missionaries to her home. A stern Navajo traditionalist, she shunned the white man's ways. Why do the Christians come to our land and preach their religion to us, I once heard her saying to my mother, Do we go to their land and preach our religion to them? If they are so sure about their religion, why don't they keep it to themselves? They share nothing else with us.

Grandma was outside her Hogan gathering fire wood, her

head and her slightly hunched shoulders covered with a dark shawl. Although she was seventy years old and getting more wrinkled by the day, she still managed to look after her flock of sheep and tend to her large garden of melons and corn. She glanced over our ways as we approached, then kept on gathering.

"Grandma," I jumped out. "It is me."

"Oh…" she said, acting surprised. "It is you, Little Bird."

I handed her the package.

"It must be the weaving material I asked your mother to get me," she said.

The missionaries had stepped out of the car and were beside me.

"They are trying to make you join their church?" asked Grandma, ignoring the missionaries. She understood English but barely spoke it.

"They are just friends."

"Tell your grandmother that her soul will never reach the Happy Hunting Grounds if she doesn't behave like a good Navajo," Mark said, grinning.

Grandma thought that was funny.

"Tell him that the Happy Hunting Grounds is a myth made up by the white man," she said, her dark eyes twinkling.

"Tell him that he should become one of us and stop worrying about his soul."

"Oh, Grandma."

It was getting late. We had a long trip back. When the missionaries shook Grandma's hand, she turned to me and said, "Tell them I will pray to our spirits that they have a good life and a long, happy journey."

"Goodbye, Grandma…" I hugged her.

Going down the road, I turned and waved to her. She had taken out her pouch of corn pollen and was spraying pinches of it toward our sacred mountains.

She was indeed wishing the missionaries a happy, peaceful and prosperous journey.

CHAPTER 5

I invited the missionaries over for dinner one night, but the menu was Johnny's idea. We moved the table from the kitchen into the living room and covered it with one of Mom's embroidered table cloths.

I wore a new dress and heels for the occasion, and greeted the missionaries.

After everyone was seated, Mom gave a brief prayer and the missionaries responded with "Amen." Johnny, in the middle, lost no time serving.

"Nothing like good old Navajo food," he commented, breathing deeply, savoring the mouth-watering aroma of rich, steaming dishes.

Mark and Dale tried everything on their plates.

Johnny reached for more. "Yep," he said, "nothing like good old Navajo food."

"Very good," Mark complimented.

"It sure is," joined Dale.

"Have some more," Johnny encouraged. He reached for Mark's plate, then Dale's.

"There are lots more in the kitchen," said Mom. "Please help yourself."

'You should never say that to missionaries," Mark said. 'Home cooking is something we don't have very often."

Johnny glanced at me and grinned.

"Had any difficulty adjusting to the food and water when you first came?" Dad asked.

"No," replied Mark. "Not at all."

"You, Dale?"

"Just a little at first."

"No problem now?" Johnny asked.

Dale shook his head.

Johnny glanced at me again. "You really like Navajo food?" he asked the missionaries.

"I always have," said Mark. "Who prepared the dinner?"

"Mom and I did," I replied.

"Very delicious," said Dale.

"Want some more of this?" Johnny asked.

"That's very good," said Dale. "What is it?"

"Sheep's belly stuffed with blood and fat," Johnny kept a straight face.

"Oh?"

"That's fried sheep's heart and lungs," Johnny added. "The other, that's roasted intestine."

"And what's this?" Mark asked.

"That?" Johnny said. "That's sheep's head and feet cooked in ashes. Want some more?" He glanced over at me. I looked away.

"Let me finish this first," said Mark. He finished the rest of the roasted intestines on his plate.

Johnny stared at Mark.

"I'll have more of that," Dale indicated the stuffed belly.

"More?" Johnny looked at me dumbfoundedly.

Dad was dying trying to keep from laughing at Johnny.

* * * * *

Johnny left the house right after Mom and Dad went to the community center to see a movie. Dale remained a little longer then left, saying he had letters to write. When I commented to Mark that Dale never wanted him out of his sight, Mark explained that missionary companions are always supposed to be together.

"Then, you're breaking the rules," I said.

"Not exactly," said Mark. "Just stretching it a little."

Later, as I stepped back into the living room after doing the dishes, Mark was strumming on a guitar.

"C'mon," he said, indicating the piano, "I'll accompany you."

"Not tonight," I said, a little tired.

"Your guitar?" he asked, admiring it.

"It used to be Billy's."

"Billy?"

"My other brother," I said. "He was killed in an accident."

"Oh… Here in the reservation?"

"In Salt Lake City."

Mark stared at me.

"He had just joined the Marines and had gone there to say goodbye to his girlfriend," I went on.

"When…was this?" Mark asked, still staring at me.

"In 1966," I replied. "Almost three years ago."

Mark winced, then his eyes dropped.

"They said he was drunk and staggering across the street," I added. "Billy hardly drank."

A deep moment of silence.

Mark now placed the guitar aside.

"You want to, you can borrow it," I said.

Mark shook his head.

"I better be going," he said, rising.

"Already?" I said. "I was hoping to take you to listen to ancient Navajo music.

"C'mon," I added, and stepped over to the door. "It's just a few minutes from here."

I kicked off my heels and slipped my feet into an old pair of shoes.

We walked a short way across the highway, turned up a steep trail, then finally came to a narrow ledge high above our home. I could see the highway below zigzagging through the dark canyons and merging with the sprawling flatlands. I could hear the cold gusty wind howling through crevices, its mysterious sounds accompanied by the distant barking of dogs, the sharp crying of coyotes and the melancholy singing of night birds.

Where we stood had been my playgrounds when I was little. I used to run on the rocks like a wild animal, feeling I belonged among the birds, and animals and the wind. Although I was always alone, loneliness had been as distant from me as the blue skies. Sometimes, I would lie on the gigantic rock a few feet beyond us and fantasize that I was a famous writer who had written many books about the Navajos.

I now gazed at Mark standing silently beside me. He's even beginning to look like one of us, I thought, studying his profile silhouetted against the starry skies. He was as much a part of our land as I was, I thought, the chiseled outline of his sensitive, boyish face blending with the soil, the rocks and the earth around him.

"Like it?" I asked.

He nodded, still silent.

"The sound of the wind, isn't it beautiful?"

He nodded again. Then, "Is...your family still bitter about Billy?"

I looked at him.

Then said, "Mom and Dad don't talk about it anymore. Johnny feels he's letting Billy down by not finding out what really happened."

"You?"

"Billy and I were very close."

The sound of the wind became more pronounced as we stood there in silence, neither of us expressing our thoughts.

"You come here often?" he now asked.

It suddenly occurred to me that this was the first time I was hearing human voices up here. How strange...

"Not as often as I used to," I said.

"Everyone should have a place like this to escape to," he said.

"When there is a steady breeze, it's as though you're listening to a symphony of ancient music," I said.

"Listen!" he turned his head my way.

"What is it?"

"Sh-h-h..."

I held my breath.

"Hear it?"

"What?"

"An-dre...a," he called softly. "An-dre...a."

Flesh bumps raced all over my body.

"It comes and goes," he said.

He was hearing it, too! Like I had been all these years.

"An-dre...a Andre...a."

I shivered.

"Come," I said, and led him away to a big rock.

We stood facing the northern end of town a mile away, the boarding school lights glowing in the darkness.

"The new high school is going to be finished in a few more weeks," I said.

"I'd like to teach there someday," he said.

"You?"

He looked away and that grave, haunted expression I noticed the night of the play returned. He remained silent as though I was no longer there.

"What about your girlfriend?" I asked, finally.

"I don't have any," he said, the somber looks still there. "I mean I did. We broke up after I came here."

I held back a deep sigh "What was she like?"

"Very pretty... Intelligent..."

"You're not sorry?

He shook head. "She's happily married."

I thought he would go on and tell me more about her. He lapsed into another round of silence.

"You still undecided about the Y?" he now asked.

I said nothing.

"You were accepted, weren't you?"

How in the world...

"The registrar is a friend of mine," he said. "I asked the President of the mission to write to the school."

Here I had been keeping it a secret.

"Dale asked Jan--his girlfriend--to find you a roommate.

"What!"

"She said if you'd come up for the summer semester you can stay with her."

Now wait a minute!

"You're going, aren't you?"

He placed his hand under my chin and made me look up at him. "Aren't you?"

I nodded.

"Want to go in June?"

He was already putting me on the bus!

"So okay," he said. "You'll be going in June. Right?"

"Mark!"

"Listen," he said, holding my hand. "I'll be back there this time next year. Stick it out until then and I promise…"

He suddenly let go of my hand.

We both looked toward the lights.

"Mark?"

"Yeah?"

"Did you really enjoy your dinner tonight."

"What?"

"Were you forcing yourself?"

"Of course not."

"Honest?"

"Well…" He grinned. "It was a little different. But a great improvement over Dale's cooking. Besides," he added, "I wasn't going to give Johnny the satisfaction of proving whatever he was trying to prove."

CHAPTER 6

Knowing that I would miss Grandma and the simple comforts of her warm, cozy Hogan, I went to spend my last night with her. As I stirred sleeplessly beside her on the earthern floor, the charcoal in the stove gradually burning into embers and the wind over the smokehole no longer gusty, Grandma slipped her arm under my head and drew me closer to her. I was already missing her wonderful, reassuring love and the quiet solitude of her home.

"You are too excited to fall asleep, Little Bird?" she asked softly in Navajo.

"I'm scared," I confessed.

"Why?" she said. "Your new friends will be no different from your friends here. The sun that shines on them is the same sun that shines on you."

"Everything will be so strange," I said.

"Are the mountains, the skies and the wind there any different from ours here?"

She always made everything seem to simple and uncomplicated. Her wisdom, however, was small comfort to a frightened girl about to venture out into the wilderness.

"That young missionary who made it possible for you to attend that school," she went on, "when he returns to his people, will you be seeing him?"

"What young missionary?"

"What young missionary..." she scoffed. "The one with wings."

"Oh, that one," I said.

"Yes, that one," she shook my head playfully. "Funny," she went on, "I have met him only once, yet I feel I have known him a long time. Mrs. Williams down the canyon spoke of him the other day. She said he is different."

"Different?"

"I have noticed that, too," she said. "He does not seem to feel he has to be nice to us to be accepted by us. He feels he is one of us."

A warm glow passed through me.

"Other missionaries come here, then return to their people and forget us in a few weeks," she said. "That one might not forget us."

"Why do you say that, Grandma?" I asked curiously.

"From what I hear, no matter how much he does for our people he wants to do more. There seems to be a restless drive stirring deep inside of him."

Images of Mark's grave, somber expressions came flashing back.

"Since he was brought up to believe in heaven and hell," Grandma continued, "maybe he is trying to undo something in his past."

"Mark?" I said, then quickly added, "that young missionary?"

"I know you are attracted to him, Little Bird," she said. "Perhaps, he is attracted to you. Remember always," she went on, her tone almost stern now, "you are one of our people. He is a white. A Christian. If he overcomes whatever is driving him to do the things he does, he will forget us. If he does not overcome it, he will always be troubled deep inside and he will destroy himself."

I swallowed hard, my throat dry and aching.

Some people are born with supernatural powers that defy explanations. Grandma was one of them. She was known as a seer and prognosticator among our people. She could foresee certain events before they happened. I remembered once watching her gazing at the stars, trembling, vividly describing images on which she was concentrating. A young boy had been lost and his parents had come to her for help. Grandma told them where to find the boy.

I did not ask Grandma what was troubling Mark. I did not want to know. Besides, when he returns to his people he will forget me--forget us. He's a white, isn't he?

"You and Big Eagle of the Many Hogans people will be writing to each other?" Grandma now asked, realizing that I was still unable to fall asleep.

Danny Keeto or Big Eagle was a boy my age. Grandma was a good friend of his grandparents. Ever since I could remember they looked forward to the day Big Eagle and I would be married. The Keetos were still serious about it, but Grandma knew that many of the old ways, including match-marriages, were something of the past.

"When was the last time you saw Big Eagle?" Grandma asked.

"The last time was when you changed my diapers," I said, not disrespectfully but in a tone unmistakably clear that I wished to change the subject.

"Ah, you young people..." she sighed, pressing me closer.

Although the young people had changed drastically since Grandma's time and married whomever they loved, one thing that was still forbidden was marriage within a clan. Members of a clan were not related by blood and relationship was only through ancestral ties, but marriage within a clan was regarded as incest. I often wondered what would happen if I fell in love with someone in my clan and married him. Would Grandma and my parents disown me? What if I married outside my tribe? A Ute, for instance. Or a Hopi. Or even a white?

CHAPTER 7

Little Bird, Little Bird, where did you fly
Little Bird, Little Bird, do not cry
Little Bird, Little Bird, I am waiting
Little Bird, Little Bird, my heart is aching.
Come home, Little Bird, come home
Come home, Little Bird, come home.

It was Grandma singing-chanting-humming my favorite childhood song. She had gotten up early as usual and was preparing our breakfast at the earthern stove.

The tantalizing aroma of fry bread, bacon and eggs and coffee filled the Hogan. Unable to resist the aroma any longer, I got up and joined Grandma. It would be a long time before I would be with her again, and I wanted to remember my last moments with her.

She continued singing-chanting-humming while doing the dishes.

Walking me to the pickup afterward, she said, "Always remember who you are, Little Bird. Be proud of your people and The People will be proud of you. Never forget," she went on "education is a great thing; it does not always make you a better person."

She, then, handed me a prayerstick. It was four finger-widths long and was made of wood with eyes and mouth of inlaid jewels bound together with twine and decorated with feathers. It was a protective symbol for a safe return home from a long journey.

"I'll miss you, Grandma," I said, fighting back tears.

"Try and bring back only the good that you will learn out there, Little Bird," she said, hugging me.

Driving down the road, I looked back and watched Grandma standing there waving, her uplifted head slowly facing our sacred mountains.

* * * * *

If I had not packed earlier, I don't think I would have had the courage to leave. In my mother's old suitcase were my dresses, a couple of Navajo outfits, my beads, my turquoise bracelets and my prayerstick. I hoped that the dresses were what college girls wore.

Just before Mom, Dad and Johnny drove me to the Flagstaff bus depot, the missionaries came to say goodbye. Dale handed me a gift for his girlfriend. "Jan will be waiting for you at the depot," he said.

Mark offered me a box of chocolates and a book to read on the way. "Just so you won't fall asleep all the way," he said.

"I don't think I'll be able to sleep at all," I said.

"You're going to like it there," he reassured.

After looking at each other a moment longer, I said, "I'll write you as soon as I get there."

He nodded, "Well," he said awkwardly, "we'll be seeing you in about a year."

Driving off the reservation, the barren red and brown flatlands gradually fading behind us, I could feel the world around me changing. We were passing through the tall pines, lush green meadows and the sky-reaching mountains peaks that

I had viewed from a distance all of my life. Now that I would become a part of that world, I wondered if I would change.

"Don't forget what I told you," said Mom, hugging me at the depot. "Watch yourself."

Watch out for college boys was what she really meant.

"Anytime you wanna I'll come home I'll drive up to get you," said Johnny, helping me with my suitcases.

"Things might be a little tough at first," said Dad. "You stick it out. Okay."

The bus went all the way to Las Vegas, Nevada, before heading north toward Utah. It was near midnight when the bright lights of the gambling city suddenly loomed before us. I was flabbergasted. So many lighted buildings!

I sat at a bench for about an hour at the bus station then, restless, ventured outside toward the glittering lights.

The sidewalk was packed and the gambling casinos were noisy with people sticking coins into the bright lit machines. I stood looking into the window of Golden Nugget.

"Wanna go in?"

Startled, I moved away from the bleary-eyed man reeking alcohol.

"C'mon," he said, following me. "I'll let you make coupla bets for me. Then, we can have something to drink."

I hurried back into the depot.

At last, we were leaving Las Vegas. I sat in the back, watching the fabulous lights merging with the darkness.

Up front, a bespectacled blonde girl was talking to strangers as though she had known them all of her life. From what I could gather, she was a student at BYU and was majoring in music. That explained the violin case.

Listening to her and the others talking and laughing, I remembered that the white kids I went to school with had always been friendly while we Navajos remained timid and withdrawn until we got to know each other better. Like now, I had automatically chosen a seat in the back while the blonde girl had taken a seat up front with the others.

The bus roared on for hours through the pitch darkness. At last, the skies in the east turned a soft gray and the stars began to pale and disappear. The island of clouds over the mountains gradually turned gold, their edges streaked with dazzling red patterns. Then, a rim of fire appeared and night turned into day.

The bus rolled on and on. We passed endless flat prairies, small towns and vast meadows. Finally, we came to a huge, lush-green valley of orchards, farms and pastures nestling between towering peaks. At the foothills was BYU, a gigantic block Y painted on a steep mountainside.

Jan was waiting for me. About my height, she had dark-brown hair and her eyes behind rimless glasses were a warm sky-blue. She was soft-spoken and had a cheerful smile. I liked her right away.

"Dale told me all about you," she said, thanking me for bringing the gift.

"I heard quite a bit about you, too," I returned. Actually, I knew nothing about her.

We did not go directly to our dormitory. Instead, we went for a ride through the campus in Jan's Volkswagen.

I was astounded. The campus seemed bigger than all of downtown Flagstaff. How would the students find their classes!

And the dormitories! Countless of them. As big as the apartment houses on TV. With swimming pools and all. I tried to be unimpressive; my mouth kept opening.

"It's really not hart to find your way around," Jan said. "Most of your classes for the first semester will be in the same building."

How do you find that building!

At last, we came to our dormitory, a multi-story building near the football field. Jan helped me with my suitcases to the elevator. As we shot upward, my stomach sank to my feet. I nearly fainted.

"We're on the third floor," she said, leading me down a hallway.

"No stairway to the floor?" I was still trembling.

"The elevators are much faster."

But not as safe!

We had a spacious room facing downtown Provo. As Jan helped me put away my things, she commended how lovely my Navajo outfits were. I noticed that her closet was filled with beautiful, expensive dresses. Was she being kind?

Finally settled, I sat on the edge of my bed and watched the sun sinking beyond the far mountains. I wondered what everyone back home was doing. Mom, Dad and Johnny. And Grandma.

"Before I forget, there's a letter for you," Jan said.

"For me?"

Jan reached into drawer and handed me the letter.

"It came this morning," she said, heading toward the door. "I'll wait for you in the lobby. I want you to meet some of the girls."

The letter was from Mark. He had mailed it the day before I left Rainbow City.

"As the sun goes down," he began, "it'll be the loneliest moment in your life. When darkness comes it'll get even lonelier. Just remember that we are all thinking of you and strength will come to you. Mark."

I stepped up to the window and looked out at the fading sun, tears streaming down my face.

CHAPTER 8

There were other lonely nights when I was tempted to pack and leave. Even Jan's warm friendship could not console me. It was Mark's letters that gave me the courage to stay on.

College, I quickly discovered, was not high school. The classrooms were large, the competition rough and the relationship between professors and students very impersonal. Most of the students seemed relaxed and totally absorbed. I was tense and unable to concentrate.

My grades were barely above average. Jan thought I was doing okay. For an Indian?

I realized why Mark had insisted I attend summer school. It was much easier for me to adjust to the fall semester when the student body jumped from 7,000 to 25,000. I formed better study habits and learned to study for exams. My grades shot up to an A-minus average. At the end of my freshman year my English professor asked me to write a paper on Navajo religion and culture.

Being a part of a culture was one thing. Writing about it was quite another. I had to do extensive research before I could write about my own people.

The Mormon doctrine and the Navajo beliefs couldn't have been further apart. The Mormons believed that the American Indians are descendants of Laman whose ancestors came from the branch of the house of Israel in Jerusalem. The Navajos believed that we are descendant of First Man and First Woman who evolved from ears of corn in the lower world. The

Mormons, like other Christians, believed in Jesus Christ and a life hereafter. The Navajos believed in a supernatural, spiritual power, but did not believe in a life hereafter. We considered death the normal end of a life cycle, just as it is for plants and animals. Our people say that like water poured into a stream one loses one's identify upon death and becomes one with the cosmos.

I concluded that although Christians have been in the reservation for generations, the traditional ceremonies of sand painting and chanting are performed regularly. More often than not, within hearing distance of the churches.

The professor was not influenced by his own personal beliefs. He gave me an "A" and read my paper to the class.

Jan thought I was great. Not just for an Indian, I hoped.

Preoccupied with studies, I had little time for anything else. I joined the Tribe of Many Feathers Club, but that was the extent of my social life. Well, not exactly. I went on a couple of dates. The Indian boy--he was exactly that, a boy--on an athletic scholarship. He could talk of nothing else but football. The greatest man in the world was Jim Thorpe, whom he claimed was his great uncle.

Jan and I became closer. She learned about the Navajos from me and I learned from her that the world outside the reservation was indeed not as hostile as I had feared. We sometimes borrowed each other's clothes. I would go to my classes dressed as a typical urban American girl and she would go to hers dressed as a rural Navajo girl from the mesas and canyons of northern Arizona.

Just before Christmas, when the ground, the house and tree tops were covered with snow, I received another letter from Mark.

"...I know it's your first Christmas away from home and it's very lonely," he said. "It won't be long before the snow will melt and it will be spring. Someday, when you look back, you'll remember that the hardest part of college was over with the coming of the first spring."

I could not wait for the snow to start melting.

During the spring semester, Jan and I usually met at the library before lunch.

"Andrea, this is Dorothy Bates," she introduced me to an attractive blonde girl at the steps.

"Dorothy Bates Johnson," the girl corrected.

"Of course," said Jan. "I keep forgetting."

"Jan says you're from the Navajo reservation," said Dorothy. "How is Mark?"

"Just fine," I said. "He's in the Grand Canyon."

"What on earth for?"

"To work among the Havasupais."

"Oh." She gave me a puzzled look. "Well," she went on, "when you have a chance be sure to say hello to him for me. – We'll see you, Jan," she walked off.

We started toward our dormitory. "She's very beautiful," I said.

"Yes, she is," Jan eyed me. "Never heard of her?"

I shook my head.

"She was Mark's girlfriend."

I found myself looking toward Dorothy Bates Johnson.

We walked on silently for a long way.

"Andrea..." Jan stopped and looked at me. "When a man is on a mission he might be get carried away and..."

I waited for her to go on.

"...Well, he might not be the same person when he... Oh, what am I saying. It's none of my business."

I knew what she was trying to say. I prodded her.

She finally went on. "Like I said, we used to date when we were in high school. Nothing serious. Just good friends. –I mean, can you imagine necking with your own brother?"

In the next fifteen minutes, I learned more about Mark than all the months I knew him at the reservation. The revelation both surprised and shocked me.

Mark, according to Jan, came from one of the wealthiest families in Salt Lake City. The Kimballs had inherited an enormous estate and Jan's father had been the lawyer for Mark's father for many years.

An only child, Mark had everything he wanted. His father had been a good athlete, and he encouraged Mark to turn out for all the sports in school. Whenever Mark did well, he was rewarded. First, it was a pony, then a motorcycle, and finally a beautiful Porsche.

"Actually, said Jan, "Mark didn't need any encourage-ment. He was a natural athlete."

Mark became the state's most outstanding high school football player. Major colleges all over the country offered him scholarships. His father, however, made arrangement for him to attend a prestigious school in the East.

"With all the attention he was getting," said Jan, "he couldn't help changing."

Mark started to run around with a wild crowd from another high school. They smoked marijuana and took drugs. Jan heard that Mark smoked marijuana and got drunk at parties occasionally. She doubted if he had gone so far as taking drugs.

"Then, one day," Jan stopped and put her hand on my shoulder, "he suddenly changed. Just absolutely changed! You couldn't believe it. He even started coming to church.

"I knew my father had something to do with it," she explained. "I heard him talking to a judge over the phone one day and Mark's name was mentioned. When I asked him, what was it all about, he wouldn't tell me.

"All this happened just before graduation," Jan went on. "Mark and I became close again. I thought he would confide in me. He never talked about it and I never asked."'

Mark decided not to attend the school in the East. Instead, he enrolled at BYU . The athletic department practically begged him to turn out for the football team, but he would have nothing to do with sports anymore.

"After a year," Jan said, "he was called on the mission."

Jan had been dating Dale when he, too, was called on the mission. Mark and Dale met each other at the reservation when they became missionary companions.

"Dale had no idea where he would be sent," Jan said. "Mark, on the other hand, expected to be sent to the reservation. If I knew his father--mine, too--, they had something to do with it."

Baffled and mystified by everything Jan told me, I walked silently to the cafeteria and had a quiet, unsettling lunch. Later, I returned alone to our room.

I read Mark's last letter again. He mentioned how much he enjoyed working among the Havasupais. I could hardly believe he was once whom Jan described.

I hoped and prayed he would not change when he returned.

CHAPTER 9

He returned in May just before school was over.
Although I knew he would be leaving the reservation any day, I was surprised to find him there at our dormitory. He was wearing the same dark suit he had on the last time I saw him. We stood looking at each other, not saying anything, just smiling.

Finally, "How are you?" he said softly in Navajo, shaking my hand.

"Fine," I said, also in Navajo.

"I borrowed a friend's car," he said. "Let's go for a ride."

He took me to a small, cozy ice cream shop near the campus where young couples were seated at tables and booths, whispering to each other and carrying on. We sat across from each other at a corner booth, still groping for words to ease the awkwardness in our conversation.

"Dale wanted me to stay overnight in Vegas," he now said. 'But I decided to catch the next bus out."

"Jan is planning to go there right after graduation," I said.

"To get married," he said. "Dale decided to join his father's construction company."

Another awkward pause.

"You're staying for the summer session, aren't you?" he asked.

I nodded.

"Look," he said, "it might take me a while to readjust. You know... After been away for two years."

"When are you returning to school?"

"Soon, I hope. I'll have to have a long talk with my parents. Then… Well, we'll see…"

Before returning to the dormitory, we drove all over the campus, then took a ride up to Provo Canyon. We never stopped and what little we said was about my family and friends in the reservation. Back at the dormitory, he said he'll be back as soon as he could.

When a whole week went by and I did not hear from him I remembered what Jan was trying to tell me.

CHAPTER 10

Jan married Dale right after graduation and moved to Las Vegas. I missed her.

I decided to continue school through the summer, then return home for a few days during the fall break. I was walking to the dormitory after registering and was enjoying the beautiful, sunny, June day when a car skidded to a sudden stop beside me.

"Hey!"

It was Mark. In a red sports car, its roof down.

"Didn't you hear me calling you back there?"

I hardly recognized him in sports shirt, Levis and dark glasses.

"C'mon." He opened the door. "Get in."

It was a Porsche, the interior just as red as its body. I stepped in determined to be just as cool. Smiling, "How have you been?"

"Fine," he said in Navajo.

I gave him a cold look. Speaking our language when he's practically forgotten us! Smiling again, I said, "It's a beautiful car. Yours?"

"I had it stored while I was on the mission," he said, swinging around. "Hang on! I want to show you what it can do on the road."

Out in the open freeway, we were doing eighty in seconds. Then over a hundred and ten! My hair kept falling all over my face. What was he trying to do? Fly?

His foot suddenly jumped off the gas pedal when he noticed

a patrol car parked on the bridge ahead. "I had lots of tickets in my day," he grinned. "Better not get any more."

He stayed within the speed limit for a few more miles, then tried to fly again.

At last, he drove off the freeway. "Let's go horseback riding," he said. "I know a place where there's live horses."

We went through acres of cherry and apple orchards, then came to a stable where riders were coming back down a trail, their horses dripping wet. We rented a couple of fresh horses and walked them to the base of a hill.

When the owner could no longer see us, Mark slapped his horse's rump and shouted, "C'mon, slow poke! I'll race you!"

It was my first ride since leaving the reservation. I slacked the reins and went after him. The wind in my face was refreshing, the recklessness of riding full speed thrilling. Catching him, we raced evenly for about a quarter of a mile, our voices ringing over the thundering hooves, our bodies in rhythmic beat with the horses' long, easy strides.

I finally let up when Mark's horse began to tire.

"Who's the slow poke?" I said.

"I should have known better than to challenge a Navajo to a race," he said, catching his breath.

"Or, to a bronco-riding contest."

He laughed.

* * * * *

Back in town, he took me to a Chinese restaurant for dinner then drove me to the dormitory. He said he would pick me up in about an hour so we could to a movie.

"I'm going to be busy," I said, getting off.

"You don't have classes for several more days," he said.

"Some other time. Okay?"

He looked at me.

"Thanks for the wonderful time," I started to walk off.

"Andrea!"

I turned around.

"I'll call you. Okay?"

* * * * *

I was reading in my room when the phone rang. I let it ring. It rang again a half hour later.

"Where were you?" he said.

"Oh, it's you," I said.

"Were you on date?"

"Not exactly…"

A long pause.

"Look," he said, finally. "I meant to call you several times from Salt Lake. I needed time to think things over."

I waited for him to go on.

"Who are you dating?"

I did not reply.

"A Navajo?"

"No."

"Oh?" Then, "You're going to keep seeing him?"

I said nothing.

"Look," he said, "you're going to be around the rest of the summer, right?"

"Yes."

"Me, too. I mean-- Oh, for! I'm not making sense. Look," he started all over. "I'll pick you up at noon after I'm through registering."

He was not asking; he was demanding again.

"Andrea! You still there?"

"Yes..."

"Okay I come by for you at noon?"

"Yes."

Jan would have been proud of me. When a boy calls for a date, she told me, don't commit yourself right away. Encourage him, but at the same time let him know that other boys are interested in you, too.

If Mark wanted to be treated like a boy that's exactly how he was going to be treated.

CHAPTER 11

I changed into an outfit he had seen me in the reservation (a pale blue sweater and a cranberry colored skirt), and braided my hair. I put on my Navajo beads and waited patiently in my room until noon. When he did not show up, I went downstairs and waited outside, hating myself for not going through with the white girl's game.

He was a half-hour late.

"Waited long?" he asked.

I shook my head, irritated.

He came to my side and opened the door. "I thought I'd be through by noon.

"Hey…" his eyes brightened. "Expecting me to take you to a powwow?"

I rubbed my beads, my irrigation abating somewhat.

"I should have worn mine, too," he said, getting back in to the car, and speeding toward the canyons.

We stopped at a roadside store to pick up sandwiches and cokes, went farther up the canyons, then turned into a narrow road winding along a bubbling stream. The air was suddenly cool and crisp. Mark kept speeding up the mountain until coming to an empty ski resort.

"You know who owns that place?" he said, slowing down. "Robert Redford."

"Who?"

"Never heard of him?"

I shook my head.

"Never saw Butch Cassidy and the Sundance Kid?"

"Oh, him," I said. "He owns it?"

"That's why it's called Sundance," he pointed to the sign inside the parking lot. "He lives up the road from here."

He picked up speed again.

A few minutes later, we came to a big isolated home hidden by tall trees. "That's his home," he said. "Want to stop by and say hello?"

"You know him?"

"I heard he likes Indians. He might give you a part in his next movie."

Big deal.

Approaching a sharp bend, Mark shifted gears, the tires squealing, the motor roaring. At last, slowing down, he turned into a bumpy dirt road and parked at the edge of cliff. High above us was Mt. Timpanogos, a blanket of snow and ice covering it from top to the bottom, a steep trail winding back and forth to the summit.

"There's an annual Timpanogos hike from the Y," Mark said. "Want to make it?"

"When is that?"

"In about a month."

"Okay," I said, a warm glow passing through me.

We finished our sandwiches and cokes, then lay our heads back against the seat and enjoyed the warm sun. We could hear the roaring of heavy trucks down the highway, the singing of birds in the trees and the humming of bees in the nearby bushes.

Mark started to laugh to himself.

"…Remember that night your brother expected us to get sick when he told us what we were eating?"

I started to laugh, too.

"…that Johnny… Just before we left," Mark went on, "we invited your father and mother and him over for dinner. You should have seen his face when he found out what we were having." He laughed again.

"What did you have?"

"The same thing we had that night. A couple in town came over to cook for us. Johnny wouldn't have more than one serving. 'C'mon,' we kept telling him. 'Nothing like good old Navajo food.'"

I burst out laughing. Johnny actually did not care for the food we had served the missionaries that night.

"…that Johnny…" Mark stifled his laughter. "He sure is a nice guy, though… He wouldn't come to our services, but he'd send a whole bunch of kids over."

I was glad that Johnny and Mark became good friends. Johnny had regarded Mark as a pushy white in the beginning, but I knew he had respected him. It was kind of grudging and mutual respect that competitive men have for each other.

"Who knows," Mark said, "he might join our church someday."

"Johnny?"

"Sure. He's not as hard as he thinks he is."

He looked at me. "What about you?"

"I've learned quite a big about the church," I said.

"And?"

"I'd like to know more about its people."

"You're not ready to join yet?"

I shook my head.

"Someday?"

"Maybe..."

He reached for my hand. "At least, you're thinking about it."

He pulled back his hand and started the car. "Let's take a ride up to Strawberry Reservoir," he said. "I want to show you where I used to catch three-pound rainbows."

*****

It was nightfall when we returned from the peaceful, secluded reservoir high in the mountains. We had a delicious dinner at a Mexican restaurant, then went for a drive up the hillside overlooking the BYU campus. Passing the homes of the town's wealthy families, I wondered whether Mark's home was as big and beautiful.

We parked in an empty lot and got out. Mark held my hand and led me up a trail to get a better view of the campus. It was breath-taking. The brilliantly lit university buildings were like a city within a city and the lights in the countryside were like a reflection of the stars in the skies.

"I used to come here whenever I wanted to be alone," Mark said, putting his arm around me.

I leaned closer and fought an impulse to ask if he had ever brought Dorothy Bates Johnson here.

"Nothing's the same anymore," he said. "Not after living in the reservation.

"You miss the reservation?"

The same haunted look of a year ago returned. "I miss everything about it," he said, his voice hoarse. "I wish I were back there now."

He looked at me a moment, then turned away.

"Andrea," he now said, "there's something I have to tell you. Something I...should have told you long ago."

I did not want to know anything about his past. Especially if it involved Dorothy Bates Johnson.

"Mark, don't" I said. "Let's not spoil the evening…"

"You…have to know, Andrea. It's about…"

"—Mark," I stopped him. "I don't want to know."

"Andrea…"

"Mark, please…"

"All right…" He finally gave in. "Some other time."

What happened the next moment seemed the most natural thing for him to do. He leaned over and kissed me. First on my cheek, then my lips. A long time. I kept holding on to him, feeling his lips warm and tender on mine, his body pressing hard against me.

"…I wanted to do this so badly that night…" he whispered. "…That night we were up on the rocks."

"Why didn't you?" I heard myself saying, holding on to him, my legs no longer steady under me.

"Missionaries don't go around kissing girls."

"Girls?"

"A girl he falls in love with while on the mission."

"Why?"

"Because…"

I felt his lips on mine once more. Back in the car, we hardly said a word, our hands squeezed tightly.

He kissed me a long time again at the dormitory. He said he would call me from his room. I dashed up the flight of stairs to my room and waited for the phone to ring.

CHAPTER 12

When he did not show up the next two days, I was sure I had imagined all the wonderful things we had said over the phone.

Finally, I called him. No answer. Desperately, I went over to his apartment at the other side of the campus. The apartment was dark, the car gone. No knowing where else to look, I walked downtown and stood under the bright lights of Academy Theater on University Avenue. No signs of him. A half hour later, I went into the theater.

Mid-way through the movie, I walked out and returned to the dormitory. He was playing the white man's game, I told myself. He was dating several girls, never taking any of us seriously.

The phone suddenly rang.

"Where've you been?" he said.

I did not know what to think anymore.

"Andrea?"

I started to cry.

"Something wrong?"

What was I? A toy he could play with?

"Andrea, are you all right?"

"Where are you?"

"In a phone booth in Spanish Fork."

"What are you doing there?"

"I'll explain later," he said. "Meet me downstairs in about forty-five minutes."

I did not reply. I mean…

"Andrea? Hello? Andrea! Are you still there?"

"Yes…"

"I have great news."

I waited for him to go on.

"Did you hear what I said?"

"Yes."

"Well?"

"Well, what?"

"Look, I'll explain when I get there. I love you."

I stared at the phone.

✳ ✳ ✳ ✳ ✳

When he finally arrived, I stepped out of the doorway, anxious to know where he was coming from.

"C'mon," he said, taking my hand. "Let's go someplace we can be alone."

I found myself being led under a big tree behind the dormitory. Except for subdued voices in the dormitory, it was quiet outside, the stillness of the warm summer night hardly stirring a leaf.

"Guess where I've been?" he said, backing me against the tree trunk, away from the window lights.

I could have screamed at him.

He leaned over and kissed me. "Don't you want to know? I went down to the reservation to see your family."

Horrible thoughts flashed through my head. "Somethings happened to them!"

"I went to get their permission to marry you."

"What!"

He looked at me.

"Without asking me first?"

"I thought you understood..."

I wanted to tell him that I'm no different from a white girl. I did not want to be taken for granted. When he reached for me, I went into arms, loving him even more.

"Mark," I said, "what did they say?"

He began from the very beginning, rambling at times, very deliberate and dramatic at the crucial moments. He had driven down to the reservation yesterday morning and had pulled into our service just before sundown.

He told my father that he wanted to marry me.

Dad looked at him, stunned.

Finally, "You two are sure this is what you want to do?"

Mark had prepared an eloquent speech on the virtues of love, marriage and family. When Dad said nothing more, he released a great sigh and shook Dad's hand vigorously.

Johnny did not have much to say either. "Looks like I'm gonna have myself a white brother," he said, grinning.

It was quite different with my mother. She objected. Vehemently!

Mark was surprised that while she had been friendly with him all the months he was in Rainbow City, she was resentful and suspicious of whites. Especially after what happened to Billy. She also told Mark about her drunken white father whose family and friends rejected his Indian wife. Her mother became a drunkard, too, she said, and she (my mother) was left alone to care for herself most of the time. She did not live in the reservation. She was accepted neither by the white children nor by the Indian children.

She had nothing personal against Mark, she said. All she

wanted was for me and my children to have a better life than what she and her mother had.

Mark had tried to reason with her. She would not give in. Finally, Dad had intervened. Although he, too, wanted me to marry my own kind, he would leave it up to me. Very reluctantly my mother went along.

In the morning, Johnny took Mark to Melon Canyon. Grandma, somehow, had known why they had come. Like my mother, she objected.

As they sat under the tree in front of her Hogan, she spoke of the differences in our spiritual beliefs, our culture and our traditions. Even if I were to be converted to Christianity the spiritual beliefs of our people would always be a part of me, she said.

Speaking for us, Johnny said, "Isn't it better for Andrea to marry someone she loves than for her to marry someone for the sake traditions? Is something like this to be guided only by old beliefs? What about the hearts of the young people? Do they mean nothing? Johnny told her that Mom and Dad were leaving everything up to me. That he, himself, had already accepted Mark as brother.

Grandma sat silently, her dark penetrating eyes gazing distantly toward the mountains.

Reaching for Mark's hand, she said, "Although the things I have said are important, they only scratch the surface. What disturbs me most is that deep inside you are not truly happy."

Mark told her that he could not have been happier. He told her how much I meant to him, that as sure as the grass grows and the river flows his love for me would keep on growing.

"Yes," he said, "all the things you have spoken are of great importance. Are they more important than the great love Andrea and I have for each other?"

Grandma gazed toward the mountains again. She muttered something in a mournful tone which Johnny and Mark could not understand.

"Yes, you are right, my son," she finally said. "What is more important than this great love you and Little Bird have for each other? Hold on to it with all your heart and be grateful that you are one of the chosen few to experience true love."

Oh, yes, I thought. We will always cherish this rare and beautiful love we have for each other. We are indeed a chosen few.

"You still could have asked me first," I said.

"I love you; you love me," he said. "What more is there to be said?"

"Mark," I said, "a girl wants to be asked."

"Even an Indian girl?"

I pushed him away.

He laughed, then held me tightly. "I love you very much," he said in Navajo. "Will you marry me?"

It sounded strange coming from a white. Still, it was the most precious proposal I had ever heard.

"I love you very much, too," I said. "Yes, I will marry you."

He kissed me a long time.

"When did you learn to say it in Navajo?" I asked.

"This morning."

This morning! I mean, what's happened to all the romantic stories I read about?

"But I've been saying it in English ever since I met you."

They were true, all of those romantic stories!

CHAPTER 13

Iknew what it meant to Mark to have a church wedding, preferably in the temple, and so I decided to become a Mormon.

Mark was against it. He said he would marry me whether I was a Mormon or not. He would, of course, hope and pray that I would one day accept the gospel of the Mormon Church.

Everything else now depended on his father and mother. As we drove up to Salt Lake City next day, I had a queasy feeling deep in my belly.

I really did not want to meet them. At least, not until I was sure he had told them about me.

"Mark," I said, careful not to wrinkle the new dress I had on, "let's go to a movie."

"Now?"

I had always thought Saturdays were a good time to see a movie.

"Mark," I tried again, "I haven't been to Temple Square. Can we go there?"

"Sure," he said. "One of these days."

I could have screamed at him.

"Hey…" he patted my hand. "You're not worried, are you?"

"Worried?"

"That's my girl…"

"Don't tell me you weren't worried driving down to see my father and mother."

He grinned.

Even a street was named after his family. And the private road he turned into seemed a hundred miles long. It was a one-way road winding back to the other side of a three-hole golf course. To my right was a riding ring encircled by a white fence, beyond it a long stable.

"Mark!" I stared at the two-story home growing higher each second.

"What's the matter?"

"You never told me you lived in a place like this."

"I don't."

"You don't?"

He shook his head.

"Oh…"

It was a big mansion anyway. As big as those in movies. Pillars and all. Whose home was it? His uncle's? His grandparent's?

Parking, he came over to my side and led me up the steps. He opened the door without knocking.

I stood there inside the doorway beside him, gaping at the gigantic stairway, the sparkling chandelier and the huge paintings on the walls.

"Mom! Dad!" His voice echoed down the hallways.

I stared at him.

"Nothing to worry about."

"You said you don't live here."

"Not anymore."

"You did?"

"Until I started college."

It was his home!

I looked around again. "What…does your father do?"

Jan did not say what kind of business his father was in.

"He owns a brokerage firm," he said. "You know…" he tried to explain when I gave him a blank look. "At place where investors buy and sell stocks."

"Oh…"

Presently, a man in swimming trunks pushed open the back door and approached us. He was in his mid-forties, wore horn-rimmed glasses, and resembled Mark. Following him was a tall, slim woman in bathing suit. A blonde, she wore oversized dark glasses that hid the wrinkles around her eyes. She could have been fifty. Maybe older. You could never tell with whites.

"Hi," said Mark.

"Hi," they greeted happily.

"This is Andrea," Mark introduced. "My father; my mother."

Mr. Kimball extended his hand. "You must be the one Mark helped get accepted at the Y."

"Yes." I shook his hand.

"Of course," said Mrs. Kimball, extending her hand. "We've heard all about you. How did you like your first year at the Y?"

"Fine," I said.

"That's wonderful. You're planning on continuing, aren't you?"

"Sure, she is," said Mr. Kimball. "Remember what your great leader, Manuelito, once said, 'Education is the leader. Take it.'"

"Mark's father has become tremendously interested in your people ever since Mark went on the mission," said Mrs. Kimball.

"Well, that's not quite true," said Mr. Kimball, amiably. "I was always interested in your people. We had Navajos working in our ranch in southern Utah for as long as I can remember. Very good workers..."

"Besides," he added, placing his arm around Mark, "It was my idea that Mark serve his mission in the reservation. Right, Mark?"

Mark said nothing.

"It's done him a world of good," said Mrs. Kimball.

"Absolutely," said Mr. Kimball. "Now, he can continue his education and get on with the business of making something of himself."

"Where's Juanita?" Mark asked.

"She's upstairs in her room," Mrs. Kimball turned toward the stairway. "Juanita!" she called.

"Did Mark tell you about her?" she turned to me.

I looked at Mark.

"Didn't he tell you?"

"Mark's been too busy with his missionary work to be bothered with what's happening at home," said Mr. Kimball. "Right?"

"Right," Mark agreed lamely.

"Juanita's from the reservation, too," said Mrs. Kimball. "We got her through our placement program. You've heard about our placement program, haven't you?"

"Yes," I replied. "How long has she been here?"

"About a year," said Mrs. Kimball. "She's really a bright child."

"Did you have difficulty adjusting?" Mr. Kimball asked.

Before I could say anything, Mark interrupted. "Andrea was the top student in her school."

"Is that right?" said Mr. Kimball.

"Imagine that," said Mrs. Kimball. "The top student!"

She looked up the stairway. "Where in the world is that child? Juanita!

"Maybe, you could talk to her in your language," she said. "Poor child's dreadfully homesick at times."

"Mom," said Mark. "Juanita's a Hopie."

"So?"

"They don't speak the same language"

"Don't all Indians have a common language?"

"Yes," said Mr. Kimball. "English."

"Oh? The Utes and Hopis understanding each other, don't they?"

"Mom," said Mark. "Andrea's not a Ute. She's Navajo."Mrs. Kimball looked at Mark, at her husband. "Oh, Richard... When in the world are you going to straighten me about these things?"

A young girl about ten appeared at the top of the stairway. She was in jeans and sweater, her hair braided.

"Oh, there you are, Juanita," said Mrs. Kimball.

"Come on down. We have company for you."

The girl walked down the stairs, smiling shyly.

"Say hello to Andrea," said Mrs. Kimball.

"Hi, Juanita," I said. "I'm from Rainbow City."

"Hi," she said, standing close to Mr. Kimball who put his arm around her. "I'm from near Keans Canyon."

"Hey," said Mark nudging her playfully. "You think you're a good rider. Wait till you get in a race with Andrea. She's gonna make you eat dust."

"Aw..." she brushed Mark's arm. "Not when I'm riding Sunshine."

"Juanita," said Mrs. Kimball, "why don't you take Andrea to the stable and show her Sunshine."

I looked at Mark. He nodded.

"Let's go into the library," Mr. Kimball told Mark. "We haven't had a chance to talk since you've been back."

✳ ✳ ✳ ✳ ✳

I stepped out of the door and sighed deeply. Jees! I mean, how could a home so big be so stifling. We had dinner to go through yet!

"You like it here?" I asked Juanita, walking with her to the stable.

"Yeah…"

"You don't miss home?"

"Yeah…"

"Why didn't you go home for the summer?"

"My father and mother, they're not living together no more."

We walked silently the rest of the way.

The stable was huge. And elaborate. The tack room at the entrance had paneled walls and a shiny linoleum floor. It was filled with saddles, bridles, riding boots and blankets. Hanging above a desk was a picture of a young boy on a palomino. He had on tights riding pants, knee-length boots, and a coat and a cap. It was Mark.

"I sleep here sometimes," said Juanita, pointing to a leather couch in the corner.

"Don't you like your room?"

"Yeah. But I like to be out here by myself sometimes."

I understood.

"Is that Sunshine?" I asked, walking over to an appaloosa whose head was out the stall door.

Juanita ran ahead of me and patted the beautiful animal. "Wanna see me ride him?"

"I'd love to."

She put a bridle on the appaloosa, and led him out of the side door to a riding ring which was about a quarter of a mile around.

Climbing on the fence, she jumped on the appaloosa and trotted him bareback. Half-way around, she let out the reins and galloped him, her body in rhythm with the horse's long strides.

I was tempted to kick off my shoes and ask Juanita to let me ride next when I heard the loud slamming of a door.

It was Mark.

He had stormed out of the house. He jumped into the car and, spinning it around, came charging down the road.

He skidded to a halt beside me.

"C'mon!" he yelled. "Let's get out of here!"

CHAPTER 14

We said nothing all the way to the freeway.

Finally, I asked what happened?

"They don't understand," he muttered. He kept speeding toward Provo.

I knew exactly what had happened. I wanted him to tell me. "Understand what?"

"How I feel."

"About what?"

"About this thing."

"Thing!"

"Please, Andrea," he said. "Don't start another argument."

Who's arguing? I kept staring at him, wanting desperately to hear him say that nothing has changed.

He neither looked at me nor said anything more.

"Is that why you never spoke of them?" I asked.

He remained silent.

"You knew they would object?"

"I knew you'd come to a conclusion," he said. "That's exactly what you're doing.

"Don't forget," he added. "I was like them before I went on my mission."

Was he defending them!

"What did they say?"

"You have to understand."

Great! All I have to do is understand and everything would be fine.

"I'm the only one they have," he went on, mournfully.

Jan's warning struck home. The missionary was finally facing realities.

"Please take me back to the dormitory," I said, fighting back tears.

Bunch of no-good hypocrites! Bigots! Two faces!"

CHAPTER 15

I was on the bus going home a couple of hours later, hoping never to hear of Mormons again.

I called Johnny from Las Vegas early next morning.

He was waiting for me with the pickup at the Flagstaff bus depot when I arrived that afternoon.

"He turned out like the rest of 'em, huh?" Johnny said, as we drove out of the depot.

I said nothing.

"Telling you all those lies…"

Afraid I would start crying again, I changed the subject. "Shot any lately?" I asked, glancing down at Johnny's carbine rifle on the floor.

"Got two last month" he said.

"You've going to get caught one of these days…"

"Aw… The deer around here belong to our people anyway."

As we approached the Rainbow City cut-off, I asked Johnny to take me to Grandma's.

"How long you gonna stay there?" he asked, heading toward Melon Canyon.

"A week," I said. "Maybe two." Maybe forever I told myself.

"What do you want me to tell Mom and Dad?"

"I'll explain to them later."

It was blazing hot in Melon Canyon, but I was glad to be there. It was home. Away from the outside world. A place I felt I belonged. Oh, how I had missed it all! the mesas, the hills, the canyons and the cathedral-like rock formations gleaming under the golden sun.

Grandma always knew when I needed her. She stepped out of her Hogan as soon as we drove up.

Johnny left my suitcases under the tree, said a few words to Grandma, and left.

Grandma and I stood there looking at each other.

I rushed into her arms.

"Little Bird…" she comforted. "Poor Little Bird…"

"It is so good to be home."

"It is always good to be home," she said. "You did not like it there in the white man's world?"

I shook my head.

"What happened to that young missionary?" she asked. "He did not look after my Little Bird?"

I shook my head.

"He promised to take good care of my Little Bird," she said. "He did not keep his word."

I did not reply.

She held her head sideways. "I was sure that one was different," she said. "There was strength in his voice and warmth in his laughter. And when he looked at you there was much love in his eyes.

"Was I wrong? Is your Grandma so old she can no longer tell truth from lies?"

"You will never be so old that you cannot tell truth from lies," I told her, then explained as briefly as I could what had happened.

"You have changed your mind?" she asked. "You do not want him for your man?"

"I do not want to see him again. Ever!"

Down the road, I could see clouds of dust billowing behind a car. It was Mark's red Porsche.

"Grandma," I said. "do not tell him I am here."

"Hurry!" she said. "Get on the horse."

"My suitcases!"

"I will hide them. Hurry!"

I ran to the corral, led one of the horses beside the fence, and jumped on. Clutching its mane, I gave the lean, bare-back animal a swift kick in the ribs and headed toward the nearby mesa.

The trail was steep and narrow and the horse was wheezing. Just as we reached the first level, I heard Mark's car roaring up the Hogan. I knew he would never find me once I was up the mesa. I kept kicking the horse to go faster. It slowed down almost to a walk. I made it to the next level, jumped off, and started leading the horse, both of us breathing hard.

As I approached the crest, Mark approached above us. He had come up the other way on a much faster horse.

I tried to turn around.

"Andrea!"

Jumping off his horse, he charged down the trail and grabbed me.

"Let me go!" I struggled. "You…! You lousy…!"

He held me tighter.

"Andrea! Listen to me!"

I pounded his arms.

"Andrea!"

I stood there in his arms, sobbing.

"What are you trying to do?" he said. "Drive me crazy looking for you?"

I tried to control myself.

"One little argument over nothing and you're gone!"

"Over nothing!" I pushed him away.

"Andrea… Please…" He reached for me.

I pounded his arms.

"Andrea!" He shook me again.

I stood there his arms, sobbing.

"What are you trying to do?" he said. "Drive me out of my mind?"

I tried to control myself.

"Andrea… Listen me."

Then, in Navajo, he said "I love you. Can you not understand that? I will always love you. Nothing will ever change that."

Back in English, he said, "What happened back there has changed nothing. I thought you knew this. I didn't think it needed explanation."

Speaking Navajo again, he went on, "Yes, I am from a world different from yours. But I am no longer that same person. I am one of you. Always. Nothing will ever change this.

"There will be times when it will not seem so," he continued. "The truth is we are and we will always be a part of each other. More than anything else, I want you to always know this."

We stood there holding each other a long time.

"There's something I have to tell you," he now said. "Something I should have told you long time ago.

"Remember my father saying it was he who suggested I serve my mission in the reservation?" he went on.

"--Mark," I stopped him. "You don't have to tell me."

"You have to know."

"Jan told me about--your past."

He looked at me. "She doesn't know all of it."

"She introduced me to her."

"Who?"

"Dorothy. I don't want to know what happened between you and her."

"But..." He seemed befuddled, puzzled.

"Okay," he finally muttered. "Okay... Some other time..."

Holding me a moment longer, he proposed in Navajo for the second time.

"Yes," I replied. "I will marry you."

"I mean tonight," he said. "In Las Vegas.

"What about your--?"

He placed a finger to my lips.

"It's my life. And yours."

"Are you sure?"

"Just as sure as I'm standing here looking at you."

* * * * *

I jumped on his horse and held on to him. We rode down the trail, my horse trailing behind.

Nearing the Hogan, we could see Grandma busily weaving under the tree. We left the horses in the coral and approached her. She was singing-humming my favorite childhood song.

I told her what we're planning to do.

"He is your man, after all?" she said, holding my hand.

I nodded.

"He may not look like one of us," she said. "Deep in heart he is truly one of us."

I hugged her.

"Grandma," I whispered, "where are my suitcases?"

"Over there," she pointed to the Porsche.

"Oh, Grandma..."

"Be with your man always," she said. "Someday, when you are no longer together, you will always have beautiful memories to keep you together."

I was happy. Nothing else mattered. Not even what Grandma was trying to tell me.

Driving down the road, we waved at her. She waved back, then sprayed pinches of corn pollen in the directions of our sacred mountains.

CHAPTER 16

I thought a wedding like ours happened only in movies.

Mark had called Dale from Kingham, Arizona, a town about a hundred miles south of Las Vegas, and when we arrived all the necessary arrangements had been made. Dressed as casually as any couple getting married could be, we went into a tiny quaint chapel on the grounds of a big night club and were pronounced husband and wife in less than fifteen minutes.

As we stepped out of the front door, strangers passing by stopped and wished us luck. A middle-aged couple, quite drunk, gave us a few words of advice, then began arguing with each other.

Dale and Jan took us to dinner and to a stage show. Under any other circumstance, I would have been thrilled listening to Tom Jones. But not tonight.

* * * * *

We had a room at the Frontier Hotel, a gambling palace with neon lights so bright they seemed to turn the desert night into a painted sunrise. I was flabbergasted passing through the huge, high-cellinged casino. Elegantly dressed men and women were making bets with one-hundred-dollar chips. They seemed to just passing the time away.

A middle-aged bellhop carried our suitcases into the elevator to the second floor, then led us down a long hallway. He opened the door to our room, walked in with our suitcases, and left them near the door.

I tried not to reveal that this was our wedding night. The bellhop must have known. He kept grinning.

"I...guess that will be all," Mark told him.

The bellhop stared at Mark. "You're sure you're not forgetting something?"

"Oh, yes... Of course," Mark said, taking out a coin from his pocket.

The bellhop looked at the quarter in his hand. He muttered something, stuck the quarter into his pocket, and walked out.

Unlike the people outside the chapel, he did not wish us luck.

I stepped over toward the window and looked out at the busy boulevard.

"Hey..." Mark said. "Don't tell me you're nervous."

"Who me?"

He came over and put his arms around me.

"My wife at last..." he said. "Andrea Begayee, the queen of the Navajos, my wife.

"Queen of the whole world," I said.

"If you're queen of the Navajos you're queen of the whole world," he said.

I, indeed, felt like a queen. My man and I alone in our palace. In the middle of the desert. Where the winds and the night birds were our companions. Where time and space did not exist and all that mattered was my man and me.

CHAPTER 17

I moved into Mark's apartment and played the role of a housewife/student.

The apartment was one of those furnished, one-bedroom deals, appealing to married couples in school. We figured that with my scholarship and the income from Mark's part-time sales job at a sporting goods store, we could make ends meet.

"Whose car?" I asked, getting into an old VW he picked me up with on campus the first day of school.

"Guess," he said, shifting gear.

"You didn't get into an accident!"

He shook his head.

"Where's the Red Lightning?"

He grinned.

"You exchanged it for this!"

"And got enough money to pay my tuition for the next two years," he said. "Like it?"

I knew how much he loved his Porsche. "It'll do until we can afford another Porsche."

"Education before comfort," he said, shifting gear again, trying to convince me there wasn't much difference between Porsche and a VW.

We planned our schedule so we could meet at home for lunch, return to class, and meet again for dinner before he went to work. My major was English and Mark's History. Our goal was to graduate together in the summer of 1972, and teach the following fall at a high school in the reservation. We were both sophomores and it meant we would have to continue right through the next two summers, carrying a full load.

Mark seemed restless and anxious during the second week of our marriage. Finally, he said that the least he could do was to tell his father and his mother about us. If I did not want to go with him, he would understand.

He understood.

The following Sunday, he went to Salt Lake City and returned late that night. He turned on the TV and sat glumly on the couch. I brought him a sandwich.

"I came home the long way," he said, taking a bite and putting the plate on the stand.

"No trouble with the VW?" I asked.

He shook his head. "It held up pretty good."

"No need to have it tuned up?

"Naw..."

Well, is he going to tell me?

"Don't you want to know?" he asked.

"What?"

"What happened."

"What happened?"

"Nothing."

Great. End of subject.

"They thought I was moving back," he went on. "I told them."

"And?"

He shook his head dejectedly. "If they would only get it through their heads that I'm not the same person who left home."

I wished he would get it through his head that I did not want to hear or talk about them. Ever!

CHAPTER 18

My wish was short-lived.

I was called into my sociology professor's office next day, and there he was. Mark's father. His influence apparently extended to the university. Appropriately enough, he chose the sociology department to have our talk. After all, ours was a social problem."

We were left alone in the small cubicle office.

"How are you, Andrea?" he said in a refined, controlled tone.

"Fine."

"I hope you don't mind my having called you here," he said, a hint of a smile forming around the corners of his mouth. "The professor is a cousin of mine."

I said nothing.

"I guess you know that Mark came over for a visit last night."

I nodded.

"Andrea..." he turned around and faced the window, away from me, "do you know why Mark went to the reservation for his mission?"

"Yes.

He turned back and looked at me, surprised. "You do?" I nodded.

"He's told you everything?" "Yes."

"That...for a while he was irrational, unresponsive, almost had a breakdown?"

I couldn't back down now. I nodded.

He studied me. "He told you he was almost sent to Valley Hospital for observation?"

I swallowed hard. Valley Hospital was a mental institution. Nothing was wrong with Mark. There was nothing wrong with him!

"Did he tell you?"

If he were lying and I answered yes, he'd know that I knew nothing of what he was saying.

"Mr. Kimball," I said, "I have a class to attend." That did it.

"I'll speak frankly," he said. "Mark's mother and I are very much against his marriage."

Was I supposed to be surprised?

"It's not only because he married you," he quickly added. "We just don't think he's quite ready for a married life. He's still not himself..."

I looked steadily at him.

"Of course, there's other reasons, too," he said. "Mark is our only child, the sole heir, the.... Well, tradition runs deeply in our family. Genealogy, if you will. I'm sure you know what I'm trying to say. You Navajos have a rich tradition, too."

Oh, jees!

"I won't mince any more words," he said abruptly. "I want the marriage be annulled."

If he expected a reaction, he was disappointed. I kept looking at him.

"I'm willing to make a generous settlement," he said. I waited.

"Get an annulment and go to another school, and I'll pay all of your expenses plus a brand-new car."

I said nothing.

"Did you hear what I said?" I nodded.

"Well?"

"I'll have to talk it over with my husband," I said.

I stood there a moment longer, making him digest it, then stormed out of the office.

CHAPTER 19

I did not tell Mark. And I wasn't going to.

All that junk, all that gibberish just so he can have our marriage annulled. Mark was more rational and more responsive that ten men like his father.

Then, trying to bribe me! I mean!

* * * * *

The rest of the summer went by fast. Whenever Mark had a night off, we would go fishing at Strawberry Reservoir.

The days were long and we usually caught our limit of rainbows. I cooked them every way I could think of, froze some, and traded the rest for venison and vegetable with our neighbors.

Mark borrowed a shotgun on one of our trips. Returning home earlier than usual, he turned into a canyon. He wanted to practice shooting, he said. I stayed in the car while he scrambled through the bushes. A few minutes later, I heard a shot, then saw him running excitedly towards me. In one hand was the shotgun, in the other a pheasant.

"Mark!"

"What?" He jumped in and sped out of the canyon in record time.

"That's a pheasant!"

"What did you think it was? A porcupine?"

"It's off season."

"Not for starving Indians," he grinned.

* * * * *

During the fall semester, Mark joined the Tribe of Many Feathers Club and became its most active member. He went to the different churches and schools showing slides of the reservation. When he discovered how little people knew about the American Indians, he became a crusader. He got the rest of the club members, mostly Indians like myself to go around giving talks. We got so involved we had little time for anything else.

I refused to give a talk one night.

"You want them to keep thinking that way of you!" he said.

"Mark," I pleaded, "I'm tired of answering the same stupid questions."

"What can you expect? Bright questions from stupid people? It's up to us to educate them."

"I don't want to go around asking people to feel sorry for me," I said.

"You're asking them to understand the plight of the Indians," he said. "The terrible injustice committed against our people."

"They were never committed against me," I said. "I don't feel any bitterness."

"It's your obligation." He practically pushed me out of the door.

He did extensive research and was quickly recognized as an authority on American Indians among the schools and the community. I loved him for it, but was embarrassed at times by his outspoken talks.

Returning home from class one day, I found him in tears reading Bury My Heart At Wounded Knee.

"Whatever gave us the idea that the pioneers in this country were great!" he exploded. "What was so great about murdering innocent women and children!

"And how did they get to own all the land that once belonged to the Indians?" he went on. "How did my own family get to own all that land?"

It suddenly dawned on me. He was going around giving his talks, hoping that his father and mother would hear about them. Yes, he believed in our people and he was truly angry at the injustices that had been committee against our people, but that was only a part of it. He was getting back at his father and mother.

One day, he heard about a Navajo arrested for burglarizing a hot dog stand on the outskirts of town. He went down to the jail to meet the man. The man claimed he had been hitchhiking back to the reservation and was hungry so he broke into the stand to have something to eat.

Mark went to see the business law professor at school. Next day, the professor accompanied him and the owner of the stand to court. The charges were dropped and the man was released.

The man came to have dinner with us that night. He told me in our language that he had spent all of his money drinking the night he was arrested. He wanted to know why Mark had gone through the trouble of getting him out of jail. The food there had been okay, he said, and he had wanted a few days of rest before moving on.

I told Mark what the man said. Mark argued that the crux of the matter was not what he did, but what led him to do what he did.

"What?"

"The years of frustration stemming from oppression. The years of having to live with the stigma that he's lazy, that he doesn't care. The years of having to live in a society that don't understand him, much less accept him. The years…"

I went into the bathroom to brush my teeth.

CHAPTER 20

We had decided not to have children until we were out school.

Late one night, I stepped into the living room and asked Mark for the key.

"Where are you going?" he wanted to know, looking up from his book.

"For a ride," I replied.

"Where?"

"Just give me the key," I said.

"Not until you tell me where you're going."

"Mark!"

"You're not going for a ride while I'm stuck here studying."

"All right!" I marched into the bedroom, slammed the door, and locked it.

"Andrea!" He pounded he door.

"We're not sleeping together tonight," I said.

"Just because I won't give you the key?"

"Because I'm out of pills."

He slipped the key under the door and went back to study.

* * * * *

In bed later, I lay my head peacefully on his arm, listening to his heartbeat gradually returning to normal.

"Ever wonder what our children will look like?" I asked.

"Navcau," he said, running his fingers through my hair.

"What?"

It sounded Indian. Of another tribe.

"It's a new word," he said. "Half-Navajo, half-Caucasian."

My husband the crusader.

"Will you let our children take my name instead of yours?" I asked. It was a Navajo tradition and I knew he was aware of it.

"There will be complications," he said.

"There never was for the people," I said. "After all, who bears the child? And who cares for him?"

"There are enough Begayees among the people," he said. "Not enough Kimballs."

Kimballs! Who cared about them?

"I want our children to be delivered by Grandma," I now said.

"Is it safe?" he questioned.

"Grandma is the best midwife in the reservation," I said. "All the babies she delivered turned out healthy."

"What about the mothers?"

"They are all fine."

He still did not give in.

"It's a tradition," I said, and went on to explain the role of a midwife.

"She's known as Awe-xai-zi-si," I said. "It means, 'The woman who pulls out the baby.

"The Awe-zai-zi-si places a small sheep skin on the foor of the Hogan and hangs a sash called squaw belt above it," I went on. "When the time comes the woman kneels on the sheep skin and pulls on a sash to help herself."

Mark remained silent and let me continue.

"The midwife would be sitting in front of the woman, holding her down. Sometimes, an Awe-zan-c-chi—the person who drives the baby out—is called to help. He sings the ceremonial chants and waves a feather bundle over the woman's head and abdomen.

"When the baby is finally born," I continued, "the midwife washes it and wraps it in a clean sheep belt. There are no clothes for the baby. It's considered bad luck to make them before the baby is born."

Mark grunted.

"After making sure everything is fine," I went on, "the midwife gives the mother corn meal to help her regain her strength and warm drinks containing herbs to help clean out her system."

"And she never gets ill?" Mark asked cynically.

"Don't mothers in hospitals sometimes get ill?"

He muttered something and turned the other way.

"You still don't believe about Grandma, do you?" I said.

"Andre," Mark turned around, "I'm very fond of your grandma, too. It's just that...you seem to have blind faith in her. Like...she knew everything that's going on."

"In a way, she does."

"Oh, Andrea..." he said cynically.

"She's a psychic!"

"How can you believe in all that stuff? You're educated."

"You believe that the president of the Mormon Church is a prophet, seer and a revelator. You are educated, too."

He said nothing for a moment. Then, "You really believe your grandmother can predict the future?"

"She can foresee certain things others can't"

"Like what?"

"Like... Well, like when Johnny was wounded in Vietnam."

"Telegram from the War Department," he laughed mockingly.

"She came and told us long before we were notified," I said. "What about the time a white boy was lost in the Grand Canyon? For days, they couldn't find him. Finally, they came to Grandma. Grandma went through some of the boy's belongings and told them where he was."

"Home?"

"In a cave," I said. "Dead. If they had come to Grandma earlier, they would have found him alive."

"Funny," Mark said skeptically, "these things always seem to happen when you are not around."

"I was there!" I said.

I moved away from him, then gradually lay my head on his arm.

"I wish I were out of school so we could start a family," I now said.

"At the rate we're going, we should be out by next summer," he said. "Don't forget to write to the school board in the reservation. Tell them we want to teach at the new high school in Rainbow City. If there are no openings we're willing to teach in any other school until there is an opening. Okay?"

"Yes, Mr. Kimball."

CHAPTER 21

Graduation was not the moment of triumph it was all made out to be.

We had been so intent on finishing school together we forgot to submit our applications on time to teach in the reservation. Our chances of getting accepted would be much better if we had experience or had a master's degree, the school board wrote us. We could have gone to northern Utah or southern Idaho and taught in rural high schools there, but I could not see myself involved with students other than Navajos.

Mark had called Dale who was now a partner in his father's construction company. Dale called back next day and told us to come to Las Vegas. Mark could teach in the Phys Ed department of a high school there while attending the graduate school at the University of Nevada in Las Vegas.

It was the best offer we had. Mark would take what-ever graduate courses he could and I would apply for a graduate school grant from the Tribal Council.

Mark was surprised when we were not placed beside each other during the commencement. I did not tell him that I had not changed my name. Catching my eye, he shook head and wagged his finger at me.

When my name was called, I stepped forward with great pride to receive my diploma. In the huge crowd were Dad, Mom and Johnny. They had driven in all the way to Provo from the reservation to see me graduate. Not as a 'Kimball'; as a Begayee, the first in our clan to graduate from college.

"College in Vegas!" Johnny said, loosening his tie. The commencement was over and thousands of people were at BYU campus, awed by the architecture and enjoying the clear, sun-filled day. "What they teach there?"

"Shooting craps and dealing cards," said Mark.

"Not stripping and rolling drunks?" said Johnny.

Mom was horrified. "After going to a nice school like this you're ending up in a place like that!"

They had arrived the day before and had slept in our apartment, Mark, Johnny and I on the living-room floor, Mom and Dad in our bedroom. After opening the gifts they brought us, including a beautiful hand-woven blanket from Grandma, we all squeezed into the VW and went for a ride through Provo canyons. Returning, Mark stopped at the sporting goods store to pick up his last paycheck.

The owner, a friendly middle-aged man, asked Mark whether his family was coming to the graduation.

"This is my family," Mark said.

Although we had not sent his parents an invitation, I caught Mark searching expectantly in the crowd during the commencement. If they had come, they did not bother to let us know.

We toured the Y campus, then went to the library steps to meet the parents of the other Navajo graduates. The men wore suits, the women their traditional velveteen outfits with shiny turquoise necklaces and bracelets. Some of them still could not get over their children graduating from college.

"And you, Andrea," said Mrs. Harris, a neighbor from the reservation "graduating in three years!"

"Not bad for a girl from the reservation, eh?" Johnny remarked.

Mom and Dad smiled warmly.

"If it weren't for my husband," I held Mark's arm, "I could never have made it."

"That's right," said Mark. "If it weren't for me letting her do my homework she never would have made it."

Considering what little studying he did, Mark's B average was far more significant than my near A average. In addition to all the hours he put in at work, he was always involved in the Indian movements. He not only continued to give talks to church and civil groups, he wrote articles for newspapers and took an active part in the Indian club. It was he who was responsible for the first Indian girl in a major college to become a homecoming queen. The girl, a Paiute, went on to win the Miss Indian America contest.

"It won't be long before we'll have a college like this in the reservation," said Mrs. Harris.

"Then the whites will be coming to the reservation to get educated," said Johnny.

"Are you a teacher?" Mrs. Harris asked Johnny.

"Me?"

"The best there is," said Mark. "A natural leader."

"Aw..."

"What do you teach?"

"He works with the young boys," said Mark. "Teaches them to be proud they're Indians."

"That's what it's all about," Johnny said, shaking his fist over his head. "Red power!"

The parents glanced self-consciously at Mark.

My husband the crusader and my brother the revolutionary.

An elderly white couple stared at us, then approached the steps.

"Do you mind if we take pictures of you?" the lady asked. "We have never seen such pretty costumes before. And those jewelry! Are they real?"

The lady leaned over and studied the shiny turquoise in Johnny's belt.

"As real at the blue in the skies, Ma'am," Johnny replied.

"Where did you get them?"

"They were handed down to me by an Indian chief who got them from his grandfather who got them from his grandfather." Johnny kept a straight face. "They're as old as the Grand Canyons where they were discovered, Ma'am."

"My goodness!"

Others gathered around us, taking pictures of the colorful outfits. Mark and I backed to the fringe of the crowd. Johnny took out his headband and put it over his long hair. When someone aimed a camera at him, he assumed a stoic expression and held his fist over his head.

"Once more, please..."

"How about a little Indian dance..."

"Can't do it without my feathers," said Johnny.

"Are you having a powwow?"

"No, but we're having a gathering," said Johnny. "In a restaurant."

Afterward, we all met at the Aztec Restaurant near campus for Mexican food.

"Hey, Johnny," Mark said, as we sat a long table reserved for us. "We have something special for you."

"Yeah? What?"

"Sheep's head cooked in ashes."

"Aw..." Johnny made a face, then joined us in laughter.

CHAPTER 22

We moved into a small furnished apartment near the UNLV campus. It was only seconds away from the glittering strip lined with night clubs, casinos and towering hotels. Mark started teaching at the local high school and took a couple of courses at the university. I enrolled at the university's graduate school. At first, it was an extension of our lives in Provo, working, going to classes, studying and spending our leisure hours together.

"If you're not going, I'm not either," Mark said one day, slumping morosely in the kitchen chair.

The first snow had fallen in the mountains and Dale had invited us to go skiing at Lee Canyon, about an hour's ride from town.

"I have research to do," I said. "Besides, I don't ski."

"I'll teach you."

"You go ahead"

He kept sitting there.

"Mark! I want you to go. Really! It's about time you did some of the things you used to do."

He looked guiltily at me. "Are you sure you don't mind?"

"If I did, you'd know it," I told him.

He dashed out of the apartment like a little boy about to play with a new toy.

It was the first time that we did not do something together and I was lonely all day.

The next time we were invited, I went along, because Mark

wouldn't go without me. I discovered that he was an excellent skier and that he had skied most of his life in Brighton, Utah, one of the best ski resorts in the country. He looked so agile and blended so naturally with the snowy countryside I couldn't help sharing the joy he got speeding down the slopes.

I learned to ski and spent the rest of the winter Saturday afternoons at the ski resort with Mark, Dale and Jan.

* * * * *

When spring came, we took our first trip to the reservation since our marriage.

Mark decided to visit his Havasupai friends at the bottom of the Grand Canyon. We rented a couple of mules and went on a harrowing nine-hour trip, 2,400 feet below the southern rim to where the Havasupais lived. The trail was narrow and winding. On one side were sheer cliffs splattered with the sun's golden rays, on the other, an endless drop into oblivilon.

I did not realize how isolated the Havasupais were.

The only access to their village was by mule or by chartered helicopter. There were no newspapers or TV. It had the only post office in the country that still received its mail by mule trail.

Finally reaching our destination, we slipped off the mules terribly exhausted, barely able to walk. One of Mark's friend, Bill Windgate, invited us to his cabin along the foamy Supai River where we spent the night recuperating.

Next day, we rode the only automobile in the canyons, an old Army jeep that had been carried in piece by piece. We visited Mark's other friends who greeted him like a long-lost brother.

A little boy about six ran up to Mark and jumped into his arms.

"William!" Mark cried out, hugging the boy affectionately. "You've grown at least ten feet since I last saw you."

The little boy clung to Mark. "Elder Kimball," he said, "where have you been? Are you going to stay with us from now on?"

Bill Windgate revealed that Mark had once saved the boy's life. There was a flash flood and William, playing along the river, was swept in. Two older boys jumped into the river, but could not reach William. Mark, according to Bill Windgate, dashed down the bank and dove into the water. For a while, there were no signs of Mark or William. Everyone thought they had drowned.

Suddenly, they saw two heads bobbing in the turbulent water. Bill Windgate ran down the bank and heaved a rope to Mark who grabbed it and finally managed to struggle back to shore with William clinging desperately to him.

"Elder Kimball didn't care what happened to him," said Bill Windgate. "He just dove in and swam to William as hard as he could."

I looked at Mark playing with William. He did many things not caring what happened to him, I thought, a queasy feeling gripping me.

* * * * *

We stopped at Melon Canyon to see Grandma before going on to Rainbow City. It was so good to be on familiar grounds again, the golden mountains, the peaceful canyons, the wonderous rock formations all a heart-warming sight for a homesick girl.

"You are not even with a child yet?" Grandma seemed disturbed. We were sitting under tree in front of her Hogan, enjoying the warm summer day, watching her weaving.

"We are waiting until we are out of school," I told her.

"In my day," she said, "we had a baby right away. If something ever happened to our man we at least had the baby."

"Nothing is going to happen to her man," Mark, having understood, said. "I am too lucky."

Grandma regarded Mark a long time.

"You are a rare man, my son," she said, expecting me to interpret. "You became the man for Little Bird against the wishes of your people. You are willing to give up your way for ours. You do many things others don't even want to think of doing.

"This is a matter of heart, my son," she said. "Not luck. Too much heart, however, is like no heart at all. It is blinding."

I felt a chill going through my body. It was a warning, a foreboding. Something she was known to do with uncanny accuracy.

* * * * *

We could feel the tension as we pulled into Dad's service station. We knew about Wounded Knee, but we were so busy studying and keeping up with our own needs, we had failed to identify with it. Johnny had signs up asking for donations to help the American Indian Movement. He had pictures of AIM leaders on his car and the gas pumps. A TV and a radio in the office kept everyone informed on the latest developments.

"How's the response?" Mark asked, sticking a bill into the donation box.

"Mostly nickles and dimes from the young people," said Johnny. "Some of the older people are finally coming through."

"Mom and Dad, too?" I asked.

"Not at first," he said, glancing at Dad over at the gas pump.

"When they kept seeing the whole thing on TV they finally got the message. Dad coughed up twenty bucks. Mom came through with ten." Some of the teachers, including the whites, are coming through, too," he added. "They don't want to be recognized."

"What do you plan to do with the money?" I asked.

"Take it over to Sioux Falls," he replied. "A lawyer there is heading a fund-raising committee to defend Russel Means, Dennis Banks and the others.

* * * * *

After spending the night in Rainbow City, we continued on eastward, enjoying the long peaceful ride through the vast open countryside. It was a little past noon when we finally approached Monument Valley. Basking majestically under the bright golden sun were huge outcrops of rock formations reflecting every color imaginable, pink, purple, blue, gold and a magnificent blending of them all.

The shapes and forms of the rocks under the clear blue sky changed as we shifted our course. Sometimes they were cathedral spires, other times all sentinels overlooking castles and palaces. Some of the formations even took on shapes of elephants, camels and distinguished profiles.

We parked along the highway, awe-stricken. We kept staring at nature's miracles, our expression of wonderment a mute testimony to all that were before us.

If only the whole world could see this glorious sight how much better off we would all be, I thought. The monuments, chiseled from erosion-resistant rocks millions of years ago, stood now as they did then, symbols of love, peace and universal brotherhood.

After driving up to Four Corners, the only place in the United States where four states met, we headed south toward Canyon De Chelly. Fortunately, we had made reservations at the motel and did not have to spend another night cramped up in the VW. It was our third anniversary and we decided to splurge a little. After a big dinner of steaks and lobsters, we had ice cream, apple pie and rootbeer floats. We could barely drag ourselves out of the restaurant afterwards.

Early next morning, we drove along the rim of the deep canyon. As the sun rose and the dark shadows on the sandy floor thousands of feet below gradually disappeared, we could see tiny Hogans scattered among the patches of corn fields and peach orchards.

Gazing down breathlessly at the gigantic monolithic walls cascading into the chasmas below, I thought how insignificant and trivial the human race was when placed beside nature's wondrous creations. Like the formation of Monument Valley, the smooth, sheer cliff walls turned the sun's golden rays into millions of brilliant colors.

Window Rock, the capital of our nation, was last on our itinerary. As we drove up the last bend and came to a summit that overlooked the capital, I was amazed at the changes that had taken place since I was there five years before. New homes and new buildings had sprung up everywhere and the streets were wider and cleaner. From the hilltop, it seemed as though a bustling new city had emerged overnight.

Driving through the city and approaching the other end, I marveled at the huge arch on the mountainside toward the octagonal Tribal Council structures and the different administrative headquarters. Sometimes, the arch was simply called "The rock with a hole in it, or "The window that opened to the moods of the heaven." The hole measured 47 feet in diameter and it indeed seem to open a vista to another world.

"Don't forget to give The Window a friendly smile before going into the Education Building," I told Mark as we got out of the VW. "It's good luck."

"Aw, Andrea..." Mark grinned.

"C'mon," I coaxed, walking toward the steps.

"Aw..."

"You want us to be accepted, don't you?"

In spite of himself, Mark glanced toward the Window and smiled.

* * * * *

Back in the car an hour later, I turned excitedly to Mark.

"Didn't I tell you?"

"We haven't signed the contract yet," he said, turning toward the window and giving it a warm affectionate smile.

We were told that with a master's degree we could teach at the Community College in Tsaile. We couldn't believe it!

Established less than five years ago, the community college was the first of its kind in an Indian reservation. Teaching there meant we would be directly involved with the Navajo college educational system.

We were so excited we talked about it all the way back to Rainbow City.

We spent the next day visiting relatives and friends, then prepared for the long journey back to Las Vegas. We were at Dad's service station when Mark decided to get Dale and Jan a present. While he was at the trading post next door, Johnny filled our tank.

"Hey, Johnny," Mark said, returning. "When are you coming over to Vegas. Lots of pretty girls there."

"Yeah," said Johnny, "that's what I heard. I'll be coming over New Year's. I gonna see an Army buddy of mine who passed through a week ago. He was gonna find a bartender's job."

"He'll know lots of girls," said Mark.

"Frank? Yeah," said Johnny. "He's a good-looking half-Sioux. He used to be a bartender in Salt Lake City."

Looking at me, Johnny added, "He thinks he can find out who was the driver of the car that killed Billy."

I exchanged looks with Johnny, then glanced over at Mark who seemed startled.

"He knows a police sergeant who used to come to the bar he worked," Johnny went on.

Mark looked away with a haunted, agonized expression.

Pulling away from the station, he drove silently for a few minutes. "Johnny's still bitter over what happened to Billy, isn't he?" he finally said.

"He and Billy were very close," I said.

"You think his friend will find out what happened?"

"I hope so," I said. "It'll help clear up lots of things."

"Like what?"

"Who was driving the car."

He continued driving silently again.

CHAPTER 23

We were barely back to our routine in Las Vegas when I got the first series of shocks from Mark's erratic, unpredictable behavior.

I had climbed up the stairway to our second-floor apartment that day and had just opened the front door when I let out a horrified scream. **"Mark!"**

He was on the couch with the muzzle of a pistol in his mouth.

"What on earth are you doing!"

Grinning a sheepish grin, he lowered the pistol.

"It's not loaded," he said, avoiding my eyes.

"Whose pistol is that?"

"Dale's" he said. "We fired a few rounds the other day. I was cleaning it."

"With your mouth!"

"Aw…" He tried to laugh it off. "Hey," he added, "if you're through for the day, let's take a ride to the lake. Dale and Jan are waiting for us."

"To go boat riding?"

"And to try Dale's new hand glider kite," he said.

"Hand-glider kite?"

"To fly with. C'mon, you'll see."

* * * * *

Dale had bought a new boat while we were gone and was eager to take us for a cruise around Lake Mead. It was a cabin boat equipped with scuba diving gear, water skis and a hang-glider kite.

Mark, I suspected, had already tried the hand-glider kite. Hanging on to the kite which was attached to the boat by a long rope, he had glided over the water with water skis then had abandoned the skis and went airborne. He had soared high behind the boat and maneuvered the kite to the left and to the right almost directly above everyone.

Later that day, he went airborne without the use of the skis. Strapped to the kite on shore, he held on to the long rope. As the boat pulled the rope and he went skyward, he released the rope and hovered high above us. As if that wasn't dangerous enough, he maneuvered the kite over the rugged terrain, away from the water. I was terrified! Falling into the water was one thing. To fall among the rocks!

"It's safer then driving on the freeway," he argued as we headed home.

"If man was meant to fly he would have wings," I argued back.

"Because he doesn't have any, he devises ways to fly," he maintained.

"You could have at least stayed over the water," I tried to compromise.

"Aw," he said, grinning. "That's no challenge."

Several days afterward, we attended the annual Las Vegas Powwow and met several new Indian friends with whom we visited. I was glad to be among our people and hoped Mark felt the same. It would mean returning to our rigorous study schedule and looking forward to the day when we would be returning to the reservation.

I couldn't have been more wrong.

We were at the opening of a UNLV football game the

following weekend when Mark suddenly disappeared. The players were warming up in the field, the band playing marches, the fans eagerly waiting for the game to start.

Just before the national anthem began, the lights in the stands went out and the announcer directed everyone's attention to the northern end of the stadium.

A bright object came flying toward us. Right behind was another one. They were red, white and blue hang-glider kites, their tips dazzling with flares. Then the pilot of the first kite circled lower until he was directly above the players. Having no room to land, he tried to maneuver back up. He barely missed the players and headed straight toward the bandstand. The musicians and the fans in that section scrambled terrified. Somehow, the pilot managed to land and stop inches away from the stand.

The crowd thought it was a part of the act. They applauded wildly. The second pilot landed without trouble. When the announcer reveal who they were I nearly died.

Mark Kimball and Dale Edwards. Dale, the announcer said, was the owner of the Navajos Hang-glider Kite Company.

Mark returned with a sheepish grin. I told him to hand over the car key. He did. Without arguing.

I went home and started to pack.

CHAPTER 24

I was about to call a cab to take me to the bus station when Mark came in and yanked the phone away.

"The whole thing was a promotion," he tried to explain.

"Promote what!" I said. "Your death!"

"Aw…" he chuckled.

I tried to get the phone back. He held it away.

"Mark!"

He kept grinning that sheepish grin of his.

"If you think I'm going to stay here and watch you fly…"

"You're being unreasonable," he said, holding the phone farther away. "It's as safe as riding a bicycle."

"It is," I said, "if you can stop and get off whenever you want to."

His grin widened.

"What are you trying to prove?" I said. "That…you're not afraid to die?"

I had heard our people talking of "willing to die." It meant that one no longer wanted to live and for no apparent reason would die. Mark, in his own way, was "willing to die." He had changed somewhat after we were married, but ever since our last trip to the reservation, he had become his old reckless self again, racing on the freeway, riding wild horses, diving off high cliffs and motorcycling over mountain passes.

"Mark," I said, "what's bothering you? You've been acting so strange lately."

"Strange?"

"Can't we talk about it?"

"About what?"

"You've never had a speeding ticket before," I said. "Suddenly, you are cited three times. And about all the crazy things you've been doing?"

"It's a challenge."

"To see if you can live through them?"

A sudden nausea overcame me. Covering my mouth, I dashed into the bathroom and regurgitated.

He was waiting outside the bathroom when I finally came out.

"You're going to be a father," I announced.

"What!" He was dumbstruck. "I'm going to be father!?"

"And guess who's going to be a mother?"

"Wow! Me, a father! Are you alright? You're don't feel sick or anything like that?"

"Oh, I enjoy vomiting," I said.

"Here. Lie down," he said, solicitously. "You want anything? Water? Milk? Shall I call the doctor?"

"I want you to lie down beside me and hold me," I said.

He did.

It was right after we returned from the reservation that I had stopped taking the pills. I hoped and prayed that by becoming a father Mark would overcome whatever was bothering him.

"Mark," I pleaded, "promise me you'll give up kite-flying."

He said nothing.

"We should be in harmony with nature," I went on. "One with the universe."

He remained silent.

"To other people it may mean nothing," I said. "You're not other people. You're one of us."

"Okay, he finally said. "Okay. No more kite-flying.

CHAPTER 25

The following Sunday, he asked me to go to church with him.

"It's good for you to meet young mothers," he said.

"Why must I go to church to meet them?"

"So you can discuss pregnancy with them."

It was about the most unreasonable reason for anyone to go to church.

I made a proposal. I would go to church if he would go through our ceremonies the next time we went to the reservation. I hoped he would let Grandma help him go through our chanting and sand painting ceremonies so that he would cleanse himself of whatever was ailing him.

"Okay," he finally said. "Okay, it's a deal."

I let out a deep sigh.

It was one of the few times I went to church since moving to Las Vegas. With all the studies and housework, let alone the ordeal of making small talk with strangers, I felt I could make better use of my spare time.

"Well," he said, on the way home, "learned anything?"

I nodded.

"Great."

I learned that Mrs. Williams has a new recipe for baking cookies," I said. "That Mrs. Filmore's husband is planning to buy a new boat.

"Oh, yes," I added. "That tall blonde..."

"Rose Marie Crandal."

"Right, Mrs. Crandal. She said she's been to the Indian shop on Sahara. 'Such nice people, the Indians,' she said."

"They didn't tell you what to do when you felt ill?"

"Take Alka Seltzer, they said."

He did not think that was funny.

✶ ✶ ✶ ✶ ✶

There was a snowstorm in northern Arizona and we couldn't go home for Christmas. We bought a small tree and decorated it together, singing and humming Christmas carols like a newly-wedded couple spending their first Christmas together. It brought back childhood memories of going to Christmas parties given by the different churches and returning home with armful of presents.

We couldn't wait until next morning to open our gifts.

I gave Mark a pair of ski gloves. And a sketch of a skier speeding down a snowy hillside. Below it was inserted: Harmony with Nature.

He gave me a bottle of Alka Seltzer. And a gift certificate with a note: *Not have sash to give Indian squaw. Give squaw white man's paper instead.*

Later, we called Rainbow City and talked with Mom and Dad. They had been to Melon Canyon that weekend. They said that Grandma seemed concerned about us.

"Hey," said Mark, "you forgot to tell them about the baby."

"I didn't forget," I said.

We were on the couch, his head on my lap. We were looking at a late TV show, but not really watching it.

"You're going to surprise them on our next trip, huh?"

"Not Grandma," I said. "She already knows."

"Aw, Andrea," he said skeptically.

"Mom said Grandma is concerned," I said.

"Concerned?" His skepticism faded. "Maybe, we should have a doctor examine you again," he said.

CHAPTER 26

Johnny came to Las Vegas for the New Year's. He wanted to see his friend, Frank, who was a bartender at one of the bars down the strip. He was hoping Frank would have some information about Billy's death.

There was another heavy snowstorm in the Flagstaff area and he was late when he finally arrived in Dad's brand new '74 pickup. Glad that he had made it okay, we took him to a late dinner at Hacienda Hotel, then drove downtown to glitter gulch, the Broadway and 42nd street of the west. At midnight, Johnny, a little drunk from the beers during dinner, cheered with the rest of the crowd jamming the streets.

"It's gonna be a great year," he said. "You two gonna be coming home for good and I'm gonna be an uncle." He gave another loud cheer.

Later, as we approached Venice Lounge where Frank worked, Mark seemed apprehensive. "Are you sure your friend is still in Vegas? He could have moved to Los Angeles."

"He would've told me if he did," said Johnny.

"We'll wait just in case…" said Mark.

"Don't worry about me," said Johnny. "I'll get home."

"Have a nice time," I said.

"Yeah…" said Mark. "We'll see you…"

I could not help feeling that Mark was distressed as we drove off.

I thought it was Johnny knocking on the door early next morning.

"I'm Johnny's friend, Frank," said the stranger. He looked more white than Indian, his hair and mustache light brown, his eyes deep blue. He stood there a moment longer, then finally said, "Johnny's in jail."

"In jail!"

From what I could gather, Johnny had beaten up a man at the bar Frank worked and the man was in a serious condition at a hospital.

Mark and I rushed downtown to the county courthouse where Johnny was held. The lobby was packed with weary-eyed visitors waiting anxiously to see their friends or relatives picked up the night before. Most of them were blacks or Mexicans.

Getting off the third floor and walking down to the narrow hallway, I felt as though I was in a dungeon. An arrow marked "Desk Sergeant" led to a wide, thick window behind which stood three policemen.

Mark stepped up to the window and spoke through a small opening.

"I understand you're holding a Johnny Begayee here," he said.

The blond policeman on the other side went through a list.

"Yep," he said. "Was picked up early this morning."

"We'd like to see him."

"You have an appointment?"

Mark shook his head. "We just heard about it."

"Gotta have an appointment you wanna see him."

Marked looked at me. Back at the policeman.

"Can we make one now and wait?" he asked.

"It'll be a long wait until Saturday," said the policeman.

"Saturday!"

It was only Tuesday.

"The regular visiting hours," the policeman informed.

We went back down to the lobby and called Dale who said he would be right over.

When we returned to the third floor with Dale the blond policeman was waiting for us.   Whomever Dale had called evidently notified the desk sergeant. The policeman smiled and said, "As far as I'm concerned you can all go in. But the prisoner wants to see only his sister."

Dale and Mark looked at one another, at me, dumfounded.

"Only me?" I asked the policeman.'

"Yep. Just you," he said. "He don't wanna see nobody else."

I went farther down the hallway where a guard was waiting for me. He led me into a big room that was divided by a thick glass wall. Several visitors were speaking to the prisoners on the other side with telephones. As I sat and waited, a guard finally brought Johnny in through a narrow doorway.

Johnny did not have his headband on and his long hair was dischevelled. His cheek, I quickly noticed, was bruised and his lips were cut. His jacket was ripped at the collar and his shirt blood-stained.

He looked at me and forced a smile. The guard mumbled something to him and stepped away. Johnny and I picked up the phone on our respective sides.

"What happened?" I said, fighting back tears.

"Aw, it was nothing," he said, casually. "Just another fight."

"Johnny!" I said, "The man is still in the hospital!"

Johnny looked at me, his smile fading. "I thought he was out."

"They said he's still in a critical condition."

Johnny stared at me, his eyes narrowed.

"They said you attacked him with a cue stick," I said.

"That's a lie!" he said. "He's the one came for me with a cue stick."

"Did you tell the police what happened?" I asked.

"I told 'em exactly what happened," he said. "After I took the stick away from the guy I started to walk away. The guy takes a poke at me. What was I supposed to do? Let him hit me? I took coupla pokes at him. Before I know it he was on the floor."

"How did it all start?" I asked desperately.

"I was drinking at the bar," he said. "I must've had several drinks by then. Anyway, this no-good white asked me if I wanna shoot some pool. Before I know it, he's calling me Cochise, Geronimo, Crazy Horse... I didn't mind it at first. Then, he starts insulting me. You know... Don't Injuns take baths? No barbers in the reservation? I never know they let you guys in bars. Things like that.

"The more I beat him in pool the worse he's getting," Johnny continued. "Then he says, 'Tonto, you chief or squaw?' That did it! I mean, how much more was I supposed to take. I told him to go... You know. That's when he takes a swing at me with his stick."

"Then it was self-defense," I said.

"That's what I tried to tell the cops," he said. "The guy must've hit his head against the pool table when he went down."

"Where was Frank when all this happened?"

"Downstairs in the basement."

"What about the others?" I said. "They must have seen what happened."

Johnny shook his head bitterly. "From what Frank tells me, they saw nothing. The guy's a regular customer. He can't do nothing wrong."

We exchanged grim looks.

"Mark and Dale are down the hallway," I now said. "Dale is trying to get hold of his lawyer so arrangements can be made to get you out of here."

"I don't need his help!" Johnny said.

"What about Mark?" I said. "Why didn't you want him to come here with me?"

Johnny's eyes narrowed and his lips curled into a tight line. He avoided my eyes.

"Mark wants to talk to you," I said. "He wants to get you out of here.'

"You tell that--!" He suddenly turned away.

"You tell him to mind his own damn business," he said.

"Johnny! What's the matter?"

"I don't need his help!" he shouted. "He's no better than the rest of 'em. In fact—"

"Mark is your brother."

"He's no brother of mine!"

I stared at him, shocked. I noticed for the first time there were tears in his eyes.

"Johnny," I said, "how can you blame Mark for what happened?"

He turned and faced me again, the knuckles of the hand holding the phone tightening.

"Look," he said, "I'll be all right. I did nothing wrong."

The guard stepped up to Johnny and said something.

Johnny nodded, the said to me, "Don't let Dad or Mom know, okay? And don't worry. When these Belliganos know the truth, they'll have to let me go."

As the guard took him away, I sat there fighting back sobs. Not Johnny! Not my brother! He doesn't belong in a cage like an animal!"

CHAPTER 27

"He's gone back to hating all whites," I told Mark as we drove down the strip toward Venice Lounge.

"I...don't blame him..." Mark said, looking straight ahead.

I was surprised to see so many people drinking that early in the morning. All the stools at the long bar were occupied and several men with glasses in their hands were standing around a pool table at the far end talking boisterously.

Mark and I sat at one of the booths.

"Orange juice and what?" the dark-haired waitress asked when Mark gave her our order.

"Just orange juice," said Mark.

"Straight orange juice?"

Mark nodded.

The waitress eyed us peculiarly and walked off.

When she returned with our order, Mark asked her if she had seen the fight.

"We have so many fights here I don't bother to keep track of them," she replied.

"Oh, that one," she said, after Mark explained.

"You saw it?" I asked.

"I didn't say that."

Mark tried to explain why it was important that the police know what really happened.

"Look, Mister," she said, "I ain't seen nothing."

"Is Frank working tonight?" Mark asked.

"He got canned," she said.

"Hey, Gloria!" the big fat man behind the bar growled at the waitress. "Get that booth up there."

"Ask him," the waitress gestured toward the bar. "He owns the joint."

Mark took a sip of his orange juice and stepped up to the end of the bar to talk to the owner.

"That guy in the fight last night," the waitress stayed at our table a moment longer. "A relative of yours?"

"He's my brother. Did you see what happened?"

"Well..." the waitress hesitated, "not exactly. Danny—the guy your brother got in a fight—he gets pretty nasty when he's had one too many. Your brother," she added, "he wasn't exactly sober either. He was downing double shots like they'd go out of style."

"Please..." I said, "it's very important. Did Danny Stanton try to hit my brother with a cue stick?"

"Look, I'd like to help, but..."

From the end of the bar came the booming voice of the owner. "...and you tell that friend of yours if Danny don't make it I'll personally see to it that he rots in jail!"

All eyes turned to Mark as he returned to the table.

Desperate, we drove to the hospital near the Hilton Hotel.

The receptionist at the desk was just as gruff as the owner of the Venice Lounge. "Are you relatives of his?" she asked coldly.

We shook our heads.

"I'm sorry," she said. "Daniel Stanton is still in critical condition. Only his immediate family is permitted to visit him."

"Then, he is able to talk," I said, prayerfully.

The nurse shook her head.

"You just said…"

"He's still listed as critical," she said, dismissing us.

When we went to the county courthouse early the next morning, Mark was determined to talk to Johnny, but Johnny had left word with the desk sergeant that he would not come to the visitors' room unless I was alone.

I went down the hallway and stepped up to the guard who let me go into the visitors' room. Johnny, dressed in the same wrinkled pants and shirt, was waiting for me. I sat down and picked up the phone.

Johnny still did not want a lawyer. No one was going to make deals for him, he said. When the time comes he would tell the judge exactly what happened. In the meantime, someone in the bar that night might tell the police the truth, he said, hopefully. They couldn't all have been blind.

I tried to reason with him that his chances would be much better he had a lawyer. He shook his head implacably. He said this is one time an Indian was going to fight the odds and come out ahead.

CHAPTER 28

There had been an article in the paper about Johnny, and word got around among our Indian friends that he was my brother, a Vietnam veteran. I began having phone calls. They wanted to know if there was anything they could do to help.

Michael Clouding, a leader in the annual Las Vegas Powwow, suggested that we get together and picket the county courthouse. What Johnny needed was public sympathy, he said. If the newspapers and TV picked it up someone who was in the bar that night might come forward.

I told him that Johnny wouldn't want them to get in trouble. Some of them owned Indian shops in town, and getting involved in something like this would hurt their businesses.

When I visited Johnny again, he said that a lawyer from the public defender's office had talked to him. The lawyer thought he could have the charges reduced. Johnny told him that if he really wanted to help he would go to the bar and talk to the people who were there that night.

Mark and I went to the hospital again the following Friday. They said Daniel Stanton was still on the critical list and wouldn't let us see him.

Dale, who had been coming to our apartment every night since Johnny went to jail, said that the least Johnny should do is talk to his lawyer.

"And make a deal!" I frowned. I was beginning to agree with Johnny. If he had been a white, would he be in jail?

Returning home after visiting Johnny the next day, I was

shocked when Mark told me he had called his father for money.

"You've never even sent him a Christmas card all these years!" I protested.

"We can't just let Johnny rot in jail..." he said desperately. "Once he's out on bail he'll come to his senses and let a lawyer defend him."

"Not Johnny."

"What are we supposed to do? Watch him hang himself?"

"He'll do that before crawling to anyone for help," I said.

Mark made a mournful sound.

"What did your father say?" I asked. "He wasn't in," he muttered.

"Mark," I said, "Johnny is determined to see this thing through himself."

He stepped over to the window and stood looking outside.

"Dale's flying a kite into the stadium tomorrow," he said, his back to me. "The Las Vegas police and firemen are playing football against each other."

"Football!"

"They're raising money to help one of the firemen's daughter suffering from a kidney disease."

What did all this have to do with Johnny?

"You know what Dale plans to do?" he said, facing me, his eyes bright.

I did not have the slightest idea.

"He's going to have a big sign on the kite, **"FREE JOHNNY BEGAYEE."**

So, that's it!

"There are going to be thousands of people," he went on. "Politicians, newspaper reporters, TV, everybody you can think of. They're all going to wonder who's Johnny Begayee."

I looked away.

"I can't let Dale to it alone," he pleaded. I went into the kitchen.

"Andrea…" he followed me. "It's for Johnny…"

I opened the refrigerator for some milk.

"Can't you see?" he tried to hold me. "It's exactly what we need. News coverage. Dale's going to be interviewed.

He's going to speak up for Johnny."

"And get publicity for his kite business," I said, stepping back into the living room.

"That's not the point," he followed me. "People will start talking. They'll demand justice. Who knows? Someone in the bar that night might finally tell what really happened."

I looked at him. Don't weaken, I told myself.

"Both of our kites will have **FREE JOHNNY BEGAYEE**," he said enthusiastically. "We'll fly in from different angles. Everyone can't help but see it."

I was determined not to give in. Not even when I pictured Johnny looking dejectedly at me from behind the glass wall.

"Andrea?" He reached for my hand.

Grandma's warning rang deep and loud in my ears. "It's for Johnny," he pleaded. "It'll be in the afternoon when visibility is good and the weather perfect."

"**No!**" I screamed. He stared at me.

As I drank my milk, I felt a queasiness deep down in my stomach.

CHAPTER 29

And it stayed with me throughout the night. I kept dreaming that Mark and I were back in the reservation speaking across the wide canyon, reaching for each other's hand.

The next day was Saturday and visiting hours at the jail were limited. Mark wanted to go with me, but our appointment was at the same time he and Dale were due at the stadium.

"Tell Johnny to keep riding with the bucking and pitching," he whispered, and kissed me.

I clung to him. "Remember," I said, "you promised."

He nodded.

About an hour later, as I was about to leave, a shiver shot through my body and the queasiness in my stomach became unbearable. I took the pill the doctor prescribed, drank a glass of milk, and lay on the couch until I began to feel better.

When I walked up to the desk sergeant's window, I was shocked. The policeman behind the desk said that Johnny had escaped. It had happened during the lunch hour just before I arrived.

"He won't get very far," the policeman said spitefully. "None of them do. There's only four ways out of Vegas."

Realizing what Johnny planned to do, I rushed back to our apartment. The Ford pickup was gone. "The neighbor said he saw that a dark-complexioned man getting into the pickup and speeding away."

I knew that Johnny had his Army carbine in the pickup and would use it against the police if he had to.

I hurried over to the stadium. Just as I pulled into the huge parking lot and approached the north end of the stands, a hand-glider kite soared into the air and released the tow line pulling it. As the kite circle toward the football field its nose suddenly pitched upward! The pilot was struggling to straighten it.

"Mark!" I heard myself crying out. "Mark!"

The gust of wind strangling the kite miraculously died and the kite leveled to a maneuverable degree.

The crowd broke into a loud applause as the pilot landed on the field.

I sat in the VW, paralyzed, my mouth dry, my mind boggled with images of what could have happened if the kite had flipped over. And he had promised he wouldn't do it!

"Andrea...!"

It was Mark. Approaching on the pickup he used to tow the kite. I kept staring at him, not knowing what to think anymore.

"Did you see it!" Mark said excitedly, jumping off and running to my side. "They really liked it. The reporters are going to interview him. They want to know more about Johnny."

I was so grateful to have Mark there beside me, I kept hugging him.

"Mark!" I finally managed to say, "Johnny's escaped."

"What!" He looked at me, stunned. "When?!"

"About an hour ago. The police are looking for him."

"Why?!" he moaned, wincing. "Why now?"

"His pickup's gone," I said.

"He must be heading back to the reservation."

"They're checking all the roads," I said. "He can't get away."

"Of all the damn fool thing to do..."

Dale came running out of the field.

"Did you hear!" he said, breathing hard, "Johnny's escaped."

"I just found out," Mark said. "We have to find him before the police do."

"Mark!" Dale shook his arm. "They've got him cornered near Boulder Harbor."

"Oh, no," I heard myself uttering.

"The police stopped him from crossing the dam," Dale went on. "He was heading back on Highway 41 when he ran into the blockade. He turned into a dirt road that led nowhere. He's holding off the police with a rifle."

Mark and I looked at each other, horrified.

"He must feel he's got nothing to lose," said Dale.

We looked at him.

"Stanton died this morning."

I felt my hand jumping up to my mouth. Mark put his arm around me, then, opening the door, pushed me to the other side. As soon as Dale squeezed into the back, Mark spun the VW around and we were on the highway speeding up to the lake in seconds.

After racing recklessly through miles of narrow, winding road high above the Lake Mead shore, we could see police cars careening into a dirt road up ahead. We could now hear sharp bursts of gunfire. Mark turned into a bumpy road and kept speeding, clouds of dry, powdery dust trailing us all the way in.

The gunfire from behind the rocks high above us stopped the moment I jumped out of the VW. The bright glare of the mid-afternoon sun made it impossible to place the exact spot from where Johnny had been firing. I dashed up the gun-wielding police huddled behind their cars and went up to a sergeant near Johnny's pickup.

"I'm Johnny's sister," I said.

"I don't give a damn who you are!" the sergeant roared. "Get down. And stay down!"

Mark and Dale came charging toward us.

Suddenly, from up ahead, at the other side of the pickup, Mark's voice rang out over the tense silence.

"Johnny! It's me! Mark!"

He was climbing up the steep hill toward the pickup.

Dale tried to stop me from climbing up the hill.

"Andrea! Don't!"

I could see Mark continuing to climb. The police down below kept aiming their rifles and pistols toward the rocks.

A couple of shots suddenly broke the silence and puffs of dirt sprang up from around Mark's feet.

"Johnny!" I cried out, scrambling toward Mark. "Johnny! It's Mark!"

"The next one's going to be right between his eyes!" Johnny's voice echoed down from the rocks.

"Johnny!" I cried out desperately, at last reaching Mark and standing between him and the rocks above us.

"Go back!" Mark burst out.

"Andrea!" Johnny called out. "Get back down!"

"Johnny!" I called out. "You have to give yourself up!"

"The guy died!" Johnny said bitterly.

"It was an accident!"

"I killed a white! They're out to get me!"

"Johnny!" Mark called out. "Listen to me! You still have a good chance of having the charges dropped! The newspapers are going to investigate what really happened that night."

"It's true, Johnny!" I said. "They can't put you in jail for defending yourself!"

"Try and tell them that!" Johnny scorned. "Instead of going to Vietnam killing people I had nothing against, I should've been here killing them pigs!"

"Johnny! I'm coming up!" Mark said, and began climbing.

A couple of shots rang out again and puffs of dirt jumped up front around Mark's feet.

"Johnny!" I cried out.

"Andrea! Get away from there so I can put the next one right between his eyes!"

He's gone mad, I told myself.

"He's your brother!" I said desperately.

"He's no more my brother than those pigs down there!" Johnny said, his voice ringing out with rage. "They're all the same, Andrea! Every one of them!"

"Mark is trying to help you!"

"Yeah! Sure! Like he was trying to help everyone back in the reservation!" Johnny said. "You know why he came to the reservation!"

Mark and I looked at each other, fleetingly.

"He was trying to save himself!"

Mark's eyes gradually dropped.

"Take a good look at him, Andrea!" Johnny went on, chokingly. "Take a good look at your husband. He's the one killed Billy!"

There was no question about it now. Johnny has really gone mad.

"Ask him!" Johnny's voice continued to echo from up the rocks. "Go on! Ask him!"

I looked at Mark. He glanced over at me, not attempting to

refute Johnny's outrageous accusation.

"It was Mark who killed Billy!" Johnny was crying now.

I kept looking at Mark, waiting for him to say something. Anything!

When he stood there not saying anything, I reached over and shook him.

"Mark! Tell him! Tell him it's not true!"

He could not look at me.

"Mark!" I shook him again. "Mark!"

"He killed our Billy...!" Johnny said, his voice trailing sobbingly.

Mark finally forced himself to look at me, his eyes filled with guilt.

"No!" I screamed.

He nodded a slow nod, helplessly.

No! I heard myself screaming. How could he! We're all going mad!

"You killed Billy!" I squeezed my eyes tight, the horror of it all now sinking in.

"It...was an accident," he said, pleadingly, his voice hoarse. "I...tried to tell you about it all along..."

I found myself stepping away from him.

"Andrea... You have to believe me..."

When he reached for me, I stepped farther away, feeling all the love, I had felt for him just seconds before overwhelmed by a repulsive, contemptuous hatred I never knew existed in me. This man, my husband, the father of the child I was carrying, had killed my brother! No!

"Andrea..." he pleaded, then began to explain what had happened.

He and his friend, Dewey, had been drinking that night, he said. It was snowing and he was not able to see the man crossing the street. When he slammed the brakes, it was too late.

Dewey screamed at him to keep going, but he stopped and went over to the man lying unconsciously in the snow. Dewey came over and poured whiskey on the man. Seconds later, the man died.

"Dad came to the police station with our lawyer—Jan's father," he went on. "The police concluded that the victim was a drunken derelict who should have known better than to be crossing the street against the light."

I began having nightmares, he stated. The impact of the car striking the man kept pounding in his head day and night. Finally, he went to the coroner's office to find out more about the victim. When he discovered that the man was William Begayee, a Navajo from the reservation, he drove down to the reservation, with a check from his father. He could not find William Begayee's family. There were as many Begayees as there were Smiths in Utah.

When he was called on his mission, he asked his father to speak to the church authorities to let him serve his mission in the reservation. It was an unusual request, asking for a specific mission, but somehow his father's request was granted.

"I wanted to find Begayee's family," he said. "I...wanted to make up to them in whatever way I could. When I finally met you and your family, I...kept putting it off. After a while, I...just couldn't..."

He wiped his eyes.

"Andrea..." he said, reaching for me, "you have to believe me. I...really meant to tell you all along..."

I looked away from him, wiping the tears streaming down my face, memories of the terrible and bitter grief we had all suffered over Billy's death just as painful now as it had been.

"Andrea..." he pleaded, and could no longer go on.

The silence that followed was deafening. The police still had their rifles and pistols aimed toward the rocks, and Johnny was waiting patiently for their next move.

"I've got to get Johnny out of there," Mark now said, stepping around me. "He's in this mess because of me."

"Mark!" I reached out, trying to stop him. "He'll kill you!"

"He's got to give himself up," he said, climbing up the mountainside.

"Johnny!" he called out. "I'm coming up!"

"Get any closer, you're gonna get it!" Johnny's voice roared.

I knew Johnny would not fire at Mark as long as I was in the line of fire. I stood there watching Mark climbing toward the rocks.

"Andrea!" Johnny called out. "Get out of there!"

I did not move.

Mark was at last at the top. He climbed up between two big rocks and disappeared.

Everyone down below waited suspensefully.

Grueling seconds went by.   At last, Mark reappeared, Johnny's carbine in his hand. When Johnny, following closely, hesitated, Mark turned around and said something to him.

Several tense seconds went by.

Johnny stared at the police aiming their weapons at him. He suddenly yanked the carbine out of Mark's hand and dashed back up to the rocks.

"Johnny!" Mark called out. "Johnny! Come back!"

The police opened fire. Bullets began ricocheting every where, the sharp whistling sounds horrendous.

Mark was now scrambling for cover.

Horrified, I stood there watching puffs of dirt and pieces of rocks clouding the sky.

Mark had just reached the top again when his arms sprang over his head and his body pitched forward.

The firing stopped immediately. An eerie silence took over.

"Mark!" I screamed, scrambling up the mountainside to him. "Mark!"

He was lying face down, his back drenched with blood.

"Mark!"

I turned him around and held him in my arms.

He was pale, his breathing short and heavy.

He tried to say something.

"No..." I said. "No. Don't talk. We'll get you back down."

Johnny dropped his carbine and came running down. He stood there looking at Mark, stunned. "Mark..." he muttered. "It wasn't me... I never fired a shot..."

Mark swallowed hard, a painful smile creeping around the corners of his mouth. He was trying to say something.

The police were all around us. They handcuffed Johnny, and several of them carried Mark down the mountainside.

When we reached the bottom, Mark was shivering, his face pale. He called for me again, not realizing that I had been beside him all along.

"Mark, please..." I pleaded. "Please. Don't talk. The ambulance will be here in a few minutes. You're going to be all right..."

"Andrea..." He tried to reach up.

I put my arms around him and kept holding him.

"Mark… Please…"

"Andrea…"

"I'm here, Mark…"

"Andrea…"

"Yes, Mark…"

"When the baby comes…" he said, his voice very weak, gradually fading. "Will you call my dad and mom…"

Nodding, I held him tighter, wanting to give life to him, helplessly feeling his body going limp in my arms.

"Mark!"

CHAPTER 30

Andrea... Andrea...

I wanted to be alone. Alone among the rocks and the peaceful seclusion of my childhood. Where Mark and I had spent precious moments together.

Mark was buried a few minutes ago beside the Mormon Church. His grave overlooked the canyons and mesas that he loved so very much. People from all over the reservation had come. Even his friends from the bottom of the Grand Canyon.

Grandma had held me in her arms as they covered the grave.

"Little Bird, Little Bird," she comforted, "your man enjoyed a full life. He knew pain; he knew suffering; he know love; and he knew happiness. He died a good death. His body will turn to dust," she went on, "but his spirit will be in the air free at last of all that was troubling him. All is well, Little Bird. All is well... All is well..." I held on to Grandma.

"Andrea! Andrea!"

Startled I listened carefully. The voice became louder and nearer.

"Mark!" I cried out. "Mark!"

It was Johnny. He was climbing up the trail.

He was released on bail to attend the funeral. The news coverage of Dale flying into the stadium and the shootout above the lake had made headlines. When one of the reporters investigated the fight in the bar, the waitress to whom we spoke finally told what really happened. Dale's lawyer, who was representing Johnny, thought that there was a good chance Johnny would not have to serve any sentence.

"Mark's father is here," Johnny said, still grief-stricken. He stood there beside me on the narrow ledge, his head low.

He continued standing there, silently.

"His mother couldn't make it," he now said. I wished he had not found me.

"Andrea..."

I shut my eyes.

"He's down there by himself."

Dale would explain everything to him, I told myself. "Andrea..." he pleaded. "He's Mark's father."

We looked at each other, tears rolling down our cheeks. "He wants to see you..."

I had never heard Johnny begging for anything before.

I reached over and squeezed his arm, trying to ease his guilt. Then, stepping past him, I went down the trail.

The tall lonely figure in a dark overcoat was standing at the head of the grave. He was holding his glasses in one hand, wiping his eyes with the other. He was not the proud, self-assured man I had met nearly four years ago. He was a father like any other father grieving over the death of his son.

I went over and stood beside him.

When he reached for me, I buried my face into his chest and held on to him.

Other Titles by Jon Shirota

Title: The Chronicles of Ojii-Chan

- Author: Jon Shirota
- Publisher: TotalRecall Publications
- Hard Cover: ISBN: 9781590954607
- Paper Back: ISBN: 9781590954614
- EBook: ISBN: 9781590954621
- Number of pages: 256
- Publication Date: 2016

Ernie Pyle, America's greatest war correspondent, covered the battle fronts in Africa, Italy, France and Germany. Then, during his last assignment, he was killed on tiny Ie Jima off the coast of Okinawa.

There have been speculations who shot Ernie Pyle. Grandpa Ojii-chan who was in the battle of Ie Jima fighting for Japan alarmingly discovers that he could have been the one who had killed the famous non-combatant war correspondent.

Title: Lucky Come Hawaii

- Author: Jon Shirota
- Publisher: Univ of Hawaii Pr; 1 edition
- Paper Back: ISBN: 9780824834487
- Number of pages: 188
- Publication Date: January 2010

In the opening chapter of this classic novel set in Hawai'i, news of the attack on Pearl Harbor has just reached rural Maui. Miscommunication, confusion, and rumors of war aggravate the already tense relations among the diverse immigrant communities, Native Hawaiians, and the American military.

As told through the perspective of a poor Okinawan family, *Lucky Come Hawaii* vividly captures the emotions and trauma at this momentous turning point in Island history, which will change the fate of individuals, ways of life, and the land itself forever. First published in 1965 to national acclaim is now back in print.

Lucky Come Hawaii is a tale of love, intrigue, humor, and Island families torn apart and reunited by the events of December 7th. The novel also anticipates the changes overtaking Hawaii, from Territory to Statehood, from small towns to a militarized Pacific metropolis. *Lucky Come Hawaii* should be required reading for anyone who cares deeply about the untold stories of the Islands' multi-ethnic communities and the struggle of individuals to find a place and sense of identity in their American home.

Title: A Navajo Love Story

- Author: Jon Shirota
- Publisher: TotalRecall Publications
- Paper Back: ISBN: 9781590951231
- EBook: ISBN: 9781590951217
- Number of pages: 160
- Publication Date: 2017

Andrea Begayee, an attractive part-Navajo girl, is about to venture out to the world of life. She hasn't decided what college to attend until she meets Mark Kimball, a missionary, who convinces her to attend college with him.

When the young couple meet and they had no intention of getting to know each other. Despite their vast differences in race, religion and beliefs they are helplessly pulled together.

Would they have continued their friendly relationship had they known that love does not conquer all, and that the past of one of them will eventually destroy their life.

www.ingramcontent.com/pod-product-compliance
Lightning Source LLC
Chambersburg PA
CBHW020525120726
47904CB00003B/971